CAST OF CHARACTERS

Inspector C.D. Sloan. A veteran policeman, Calleshire born and bred.

Detective-Constable William Crosby. Unlettered and a bit raw, but not without potential.

The Mother Superior. A calm woman of immense authority who presides over the Convent of St. Anselm.

Sister Lucy. Her right-hand woman, the convent bursar and procuratrix.

Sister Peter. The young, nervous chantress, who finds blood on her hand.

Sister Damien. Angular, intense and exceedingly devout, she is obsessed with the desire to see the convent obtain the funds to build a cloister.

Sister Anne. The murder victim. In her past life she was Josephine Mary Cartwright, possibly an heir to the lucrative family business.

Sister Polycarp. Elderly, gruff, and Irish, she is the convent gatekeeper.

Father Benedict MacAuley. The local priest, a frequent convent visitor.

Hobbett. The convent handyman, who does as little as possible.

Harold Cartwright. Sister Anne's cousin, who won't say why he is visiting the convent. He manages Cartwright's Consolidated Carbons.

Marwin Ranby. Principal of the Agricultural Institute across the way.

Celia Feine. His fiancee, whose wealthy family once owned the edifice that now houses St. Anselm's.

William Tewn. A student at the Institute and ringleader in an unfortunate Guy Fawkes prank with tragic consequences.

Sergeant Polly Perkins. A lively and dedicated young police officer.

Superintendent Leeyes. Sloan's boss, a man bent on self-improvement.

Dr. Dabbe. The capable police pathologist.

Plus assorted nuns, policemen, and family members.

Books by Catherine Aird
(all featuring Inspector Sloan with the exception of
A Most Contagious Game)

The Religious Body (1966)
A Most Contagious Game (1967)
Henrietta Who? (1968)
The Complete Steel (1969)
(*The Stately Home Murder* in the U.S.)
A Late Phoenix (1970)
His Burial Too (1973)
Slight Mourning (1975)
Parting Breath (1977)
Some Die Eloquent (1979)
Passing Strange (1980)
Last Respects (1982)
Harm's Way (1984)
A Dead Liberty (1986)
The Body Politic (1990)
A Going Concern (1993)
Injury Time (1994 , short stories
featuring Sloan and others)
After Effects (1996)
Stiff News (1998)
Little Knell (2001)
Amendment Of Life (2003)
Chapter And Hearse (2004 , short stories
featuring Sloan and others)
A Hole in One (2005)

THE RELIGIOUS BODY

BY CATHERINE AIRD

Boulder / Lyons
Rue Morgue Press

All of the characters in this book are fictitious,
and any resemblance to actual persons,
living or dead, is purely coincidental.

The quotation from The Stately Homes of England *on
page 134 is printed by permission of Mr. Noël Coward
and Chappell and Company Limited.*

THE RELIGIOUS BODY
978-1-60187-012-4
All rights reserved.
Copyright © 1966 by Catherine Aird.
New material copyright © 2007
by The Rue Morgue Press
87 Lone Tree Lane
Lyons, CO 80540

Printed by
Johnson Printing
Boulder, Colorado

PRINTED IN THE UNITED STATES OF AMERICA

For my parents, with love

"What I want to know is:
One—who is the criminal?
Two—how did he (or she) do it?"

—Ernest the Policeman,
in *The Toytown Mystery*
by S. G. Hulme Beaman.

About Catherine Aird

Catherine Aird's first book, *The Religious Body* (1966), features, as does all of her subsequent novels, Inspector C.D. Sloan of the Calleshire C.I.D. You won't find Calleshire in any atlas. Like Anthony Trollope (followed by Angela Thirkell) and later Thomas Hardy, Aird chose to create an imaginary shire in which to set her stories, partly "so that it could have all the usual institutions without my having to worry about upsetting real people." Calleshire, however, no doubt in many ways resembles Kent, where Catherine Aird, a pseudonym for Kinn Hamilton McIntosh, born in Yorkshire in 1930, has made her home in a small village near Canterbury for most of her life, living in the same house since 1946. "Real life (and) that intimate knowledge of the same English village" has provided Aird with most of the background needed for her books. She suspects that her fellow villagers rarely think of her as a writer and are more likely to refer to her as the village doctor's daughter, a onetime golfer, and as an editor and publisher of village histories. She neglects to add that her neighbors might also have noticed that she was made an M.B.E. for her longtime work with the Girl Guides Association.

Some English critics, T.J. Binyon, for example, have grumbled that "it is difficult to create a sense of place with an imaginary locality" while grudgingly admitting that her books are "nicely contrived and pleasantly unpretentious." What Binyon fails to understand is that the majority of mystery readers, especially Americans, are more interested in a somewhat idealized English landscape than in the frequently blighted real thing.

Aird did not start out to be a writer. She intended to follow in her father's footsteps and study medicine but had to abandon that idea when she came down with nephrotic syndrome, a very serious condition that often leads to kidney failure. It's less lethal today, thanks to steroids and transplants, but more than a half century ago it forced her to take to bed for an extended period, during which she read a great deal of detective fiction, including Sapper, the Saint, Raymond Chandler, and, of course, one of her personal favorites, Josephine Tey, whose own *Daughter of Time* also explores an historical mystery with the detective having to resort to research to solve a long-ago crime. Later she wrote "two or three bad novels before turning to crime so to speak—definitely a case of poacher turned gamekeeper."

Grounded as she was in the traditional mystery, it's not surprising that her books reflect many of the aspects of mysteries from the Golden Age of detection (roughly 1913 to 1953) when fair play was the name of the game and the reader an active participant in uncovering whodunit. Such a reader was Aird's mother, who would faithfully read the first couple of chapters of her daughter's manuscripts, jot down the name of the villain and then place this piece of paper in a sealed envelope to be opened when the book was done. Her mother figured out the villain every time. "Fine words, carefully crafted by me to conceal the murderer among a welter of more suspicious characters, buttered no parsnips with her," writes Aird.

Aird's entry into the ranks of crime writers was warmly welcomed by the critics. Crime fiction historian Melvyn Barnes cited her as one of the writers who "has breathed new life into the genre, concentrating mainly upon the cosy village puzzle of the golden age tradition but showing welcome unwillingness to maintain the rather colorless, unconvincing and formulaic approach of so many of her predecessors...those who say that the modern crime novel heralded the demise of the traditional mystery story will continue to be confounded by writers of Catherine Aird's standard." Her third book—and second Sloan—*Henrietta Who?* (1968) was picked by *New York Times* reviewer Allen J. Hubin as one of the best books of the year. In discussing her work in the *St. James Guide to Crime and Mystery Writers*, Pearl G. Aldrich said Aird was a throwback to "the leisurely, kinder, gentler crime novel.," displaying a tone that "is smiling, good-natured, good-mannered, (and) amusing." Aldrich points out that the "voice of the omniscient author is heard continuously, commenting, explaining, digressing, joking, adding extraneous information, and explaining English ways and attitudes." Aldrich is especially fond of *The Complete Steel*, published in the U.S. as *The Stately Home Murder* (1969). Easily the funniest book in Aird's output, the action focuses on a dotty titled family struggling to make ends meet. In 2002, this title was one of 103 mysteries chosen for inclusion in *They Died in Vain: Overlooked,*

Underappreciated and Forgotten Mystery Novels, edited by Jim Huang with contributions from members of the Independent Mystery Booksellers Association.

For more information on Aird (and her one non-Sloan novel) see Tom & Enid Schantz' introduction to The Rue Morgue Press edition of A Most Contagious Game, from which this note on the author was excerpted.

THE RELIGIOUS BODY

CHAPTER ONE

Sister Mary St. Gertrude put out a hand and stilled the tiny alarm clock long before it got into its stride. It was five o'clock and quite dark. She slipped quickly out of bed, shivering a little. The Convent of St. Anselm wasn't completely unheated but at five o'clock on a November morning it felt as if it was.

She dressed very quietly, splashing some cold water on her face from a basin in the corner of the little room. The water was really chilled and she dressed even more quickly afterwards. Her habit complete, she knelt at the *prie-dieu* in front of the window and made her first private devotions of the day. Then she drew back the curtains of the window and stripped off her bed.

It was then twenty-five minutes past five. Utterly used to a day ordained by a combination of tradition and the clock, she picked up her breviary and read therein for exactly five minutes. As the hands of the clock crept round to the half-hour she closed the book and slipped out of the door. It was Sister Gertrude's duty this month to awake the Convent.

She herself slept on the top landing of the house and she went first of all to pull back those landing curtains. Half a mile away the village of Cullingoak still slept on in darkness. There was just one light visible from where she stood and that was in the bakery. It would be another half an hour before the next light appeared—in the newspaper shop, where the day's complement of disaster and gossip arrived from Berebury by van.

Sister Gertrude arranged the drawn curtains neatly at the sides of the window and turned away. Newspapers had not been one of the things she had regretted when she left the world.

She descended to the landing below and drew back another set of curtains on the other side of the house. In this direction, a couple of fields away, lay the Cullingoak Agricultural Institute. It, too, was invisible in the darkness, but presently the boy who was duty herdsman for the week would start the milking. Occasionally in the Convent they could hear the lowing of the cattle as they moved slowly across the fields. Sister Gertrude turned down a corridor, counting the doors as she passed them. Six, five, fo … four. At four doors away there was no mistaking Sister Mary St. Hilda's snore.

It rose to an amazing crescendo and then stopped with disturbing suddenness—only to start seconds later working its way up to a new climax. Sister Bonaventure called it the Convent's answer to the Institute's cows, but then Sister Bonaventure declared the snore could be heard six doors away on a good day.

She may well have been right. It was true that the only person in the Convent of St. Anselm who didn't know about Sister Hilda's snore was Sister Hilda. It was, thought Sister Gertrude wryly, a true test of religious behavior to sleep uncomplainingly up to four—or even five—doors away from her, and greet the cheerful unknowing Sister Hilda with true Christian charity each morning. She had had to do it herself and she knew. But how she had longed to be able to go in and turn her over onto her other side.

She wished now that she could wake her first but there was a prescribed order for this as there was for everything else in convent life. It was decreed that the first door on which she had to knock every morning was that of the Reverend Mother. Why this was so, she did not know. It may have been because it was unthinkable that the Mother Superior should sleep while any of her daughters in religion were awake. It may have been one of the things—one of the many things—whose origin was lost in the dim antiquity when their Order was founded.

She had to go round two more corners before she came to the Reverend Mother's door. She tapped gently.

"I ask your blessing, Mother."

"God bless you, my daughter." The answer came swiftly through the door in a deep, calm voice. She never had to knock twice to wake the Reverend Mother.

The next door on which she had to knock was that of the Sacrist. She must always be up betimes.

"God bless you, Sister."

"God bless *you*, Sister," responded the Sacrist promptly.

Then the Cellarer. She, too, had early work to do.

"God bless you, Sister."

And the Novice Mistress.

No response.

Another knock, louder.

"God bless you, Sister," sleepily. The Novice Mistress sounded as if she had been hauled back from a pleasant dream.

The Bursar and Procuratrix, the Mother Superior's right-hand woman Sister Lucy.

"God bless you, Sister." No delay here. She sounded very wide awake.

Then she could start on the ordinary doors, one after the other. There were still fifty to go.

Knock.

"God bless you, Sister," tentatively.

The unmistakable sound of dentures being seized from a tin mug.

Pause.

Then, triumphantly, "God bless *you*, Sister."

Knock, blessing, response. Knock, blessing, response.

In a way the formula made the job easier. "Half past five on a November morning and all's well" doubtless would have its uses, but hardly in a Convent. She drew back yet another set of landing curtains and was glad she didn't have to say something about the weather fifty-five times every morning. It wasn't a particularly nice morning but not bad for November, not bad at all. It looked as if it would stay fine for tonight, which was Bonfire Night. Sister Gertrude had not been so long out of the world that she couldn't remember the importance to children of having a fine night for their fires. Besides, a damp November Fifth was a sore trial to everyone—then you never knew when they would let their fireworks off. She wondered what the students at the Agricultural Institute were planning. Last year they had burnt down the old bus shelter in the center of the village. Not before time, she had been told, and now there was a brand new one there.

Knock, blessing, response. Knock, blessing, response.

The older the Sister, the quicker the response. Sister Gertrude had worked that out long ago. She called the older ones first—partly because they slept on the lower floors, partly because she could still remember how much those extra minutes' sleep had meant when she was a young nun. Sleep had been a most precious commodity then.

Knock, blessing, unintelligible response. That was old Mother Mary St. Thérèse, aged goodness knows what, professed long before Sister Gertrude was born, with a memory like a set of archives. Woe betide any Reverend Mother with an eye for innovation. Mother Thérèse had outlived a string of Prioresses, each of whom, she managed to infer (without any apparent lapse of Christian charity), was not a patch on their predecessor. There were days now when she was not able to leave her room. The Reverend Mother would visit her then, and listen patiently to interminable recitations of the virtues of Mother Helena of blessed memory, in whose time it seemed life in the Convent of St. Anselm had been perfect.

Knock, blessing, response.

She turned back into the corridor where Sister Hilda was the soundest sleeper. The snore was still rising and falling "like all the trumpets," thought Sister Gertrude, before she realized that it was an irreverent simile, and that custody of the mind was just as important as custody of the eyes even if it was half past five in the morning and she was all alone in the dim corridor.

Knock, blessing, response.

That was the door next to Sister Hilda, Sister Jerome. Sister Gertrude wondered what sort of a night she had had. Perhaps the snore didn't bother her, but if it did, she couldn't very well say, not after solemnly undertaking to live at peace for ever with her Sisters in religion.

Knock, blessing, response.

Sister Hilda's door.

The snore ground to a halt, there were a couple of choking snorts, and then the pleasant voice of Sister Hilda sang out warmly, "God bless *you*, Sister."

It was strange but true that Sister Hilda had one of the most mellifluous speaking voices in the Convent. Sister Gertrude shook her head at this phenomenon and passed on to the next door.

Knock, blessing … no response.

Knock (louder), blessing (more insistently) … still no response.

Sister Anne's teeth were her own. She could think of no other reason for delay in answering and put her hand on the door: the room was empty, the bed made. A very human grin spread over Sister Gertrude's face. Sister Anne hadn't been able to stick another minute of that snore and had crept down early. Strictly forbidden, of course. So was making your bed to save dashing up before Sext. She made a mental note to pull her leg about that later, and, taking a look at her watch, hurried along to the next door. There was still the entire novitiate to be woken, to say nothing of a row of postulants—and *they* never wanted to get up.

At ten minutes to six Sister Gertrude slipped into her stall in the quiet Chapel and went down on her knees until the service began. There was no formal procession into the Chapel for this service. Each Sister came to her own stall and knelt until the stroke of six. She heard the crunch of car wheels on the gravel outside. That was Father MacAuley come to take the service. She lowered her head. She was glad enough to kneel peacefully, her first task of the day completed. Gradually in the few minutes before the service she emptied her mind of all but prayer and worship, and as the ancient ritual proceeded she was oblivious of everything save the proper order of bidding and response.

Until Sister Peter moved forward.

Sister Peter was Chantress, which office weighed heavily on her slight shoulders. She was young still and inclined to start nervously when spoken to.

After the Epistle she stepped into the aisle and walked up to the altar steps for an antiphon. Her music manuscript—hand-illuminated and old— was there, ready open on its stand.

The Sisters rose, their eyes on the Chantress, waiting for her to start the Gradual.

Sister Peter's voice gave them the note, and the antiphon began. The Sisters sang their way through the time-honored phrases. On the steps of the altar, Sister Peter put out her right hand to turn the music manuscript over, touched it—and shot back as if she had been stung.

The nuns sang on.

Sister Peter's face paled visibly. She stared first at the manuscript and then at her own hand. It was as if she could not believe what she saw there. She went on staring at the manuscript. She made no attempt to turn the page over but stood there in front of the stand, an incredulous expression on her face, until the nuns had sung their own way to the end of the Gradual.

Then she genuflected deeply and turned and walked back to her stall, her face a troubled, tragic white, her hands clasped together in front of her but nevertheless visibly trembling.

The congregation settled themselves for the Gospel.

Convent life, reflected Sister Gertrude, was never without interest.

They filed out of the Chapel in twos, hands clasped together in front, bowing to the altar. They proceeded to the refectory where they bowed to the Abbatial chair and then stood, backs to their own benches, while grace was said.

"Amen," said the Community in unison.

There was a rustle of habits and then the nuns were seated. One sat apart on a little dais, a reading desk in front of her. When all was still she began to read aloud from the Martyrology. The Refectarian stood by the serving hatch, her eye on the Reverend Mother. The Reader started to detail the sufferings of the early Christian martyrs. At the end of the first page she paused. The Reverend Mother knocked once on the table. The serving hatch flew up and the Refectarian seized an enormous teapot, set it down at a table and went back for another. A young Sister appeared with the first of several baskets of bread. This was passed rapidly down one of the long tables.

The incredible tortures inflicted on the martyrs were obscured by the crunching of crusts and the sipping of hot tea. The Reader raised her voice to tell of boiling oil and decapitation. The teapot went on its second round, the bread baskets emptied. Only little Sister Peter seemed to be with the Reader completely. Her expression would have brought satisfaction to any torturer.

It was at this point that Sister Gertrude noticed the empty place. It was between Sister Damien, angular, intense and exceedingly devout, and Sister Michael, plumpish, placid and more than a little deaf. Sister Anne's place. She must have been taken ill in the night and whisked off to the Convent's tiny sick bay. Sister Gertrude's glance slid along the bench to where the austere figure of Sister Radigund, the Infirmarium, was sitting. She would ask her at the end of the General Silence.

The morning's quota of bread and tea came to an end. The Reader was tidying up the remains of the dismembered martyrs in a general "And in other places and at other times of many other martyrs, confessors and holy virgins to whose prayers and merits we humbly commend ourselves."

"Deo gratias," responded the Community.

At this moment Sister Peter rose, bowed to the Mother Superior and went slowly round the table to stand in front of the Abbatial chair. The Mother Superior looked up at her and nodded. Sister Peter went down on her knees and clasped her hands together in front of her.

"I confess my fault," began Sister Peter in a voice that was far from steady, "to God and to you, Mother Abbess, and to all the Sisters that I have committed the great sin of damaging the Gradual ..." There was an indrawing of breaths that would have done credit to a chorus in their unity. "... by placing a thumb mark on it," went on Sister Peter bravely. "For this and all my other faults and those I have occasioned in others, I humbly ask pardon of God and penance of you, Mother Abbess, for the love of God." She finished in a rush and knelt there, eyes cast down.

The Reverend Mother considered the kneeling figure. "May the Lord forgive you your faults, my dear child, and give you grace to be faithful to grace. Say a *Miserere* and ..." she paused and looked across the room, "... and ask Sister Jerome if she will take a look at the mark quickly. It may be possible to remove it without lasting damage."

In the general bustle and end of silence after breakfast, Sister Gertrude sought out Sister Radigund.

"Sister Anne? She's not ill that I know of. She might have gone to the sick bay on her own, of course, though it's not usual. ..."

It was expressly forbidden as it happened, but it would have been uncharitable of Sister Radigund to have said so.

"... I'll go up after Office if you like, to make sure."

"Thank you," said Sister Gertrude gratefully. She wondered now if she should have reported the empty bedroom. Her mind was more on that than on Sext, and afterwards she waited anxiously at the bottom of the staircase for Sister Radigund.

"She's not in the sick bay," said the Infirmarium, "nor back in her own cell either. I've just checked."

"I think," said Sister Gertrude, "that we'd better go to the Parlor, don't you?"

They were not the only Sisters waiting at the Reverend Mother's door. Sister Jerome, the Convent's most skilled authority on manuscript illumination, and Sister Peter were both there too. They knocked and a little bell rang. Sister Gertrude sighed. That was where the world and the Convent differed so. In the Convent to every sound and every speech there was a response. In the world—well ...

The four Sisters trooped in. The Mother Superior was working on the morning's post with Sister Lucy, the Bursar. There were several neat piles of paper on the table, and Sister Lucy was bending over a notebook.

The Mother Superior looked up briskly.

"Ah, yes, Sister Peter. The mark on the Gradual. I'm sure that Sister Jerome will be able to remove it, whatever it is. These culpable faults are all very well but we can't have you—er—making a meal of them, can we? Otherwise they become an indulgence in themselves and that would never do." She gave a quick smile. "Isn't that so, Sister Jerome? Now, stop looking like a Tragedy Queen and go back to …"

Sister Peter burst into tears. "That's just it, Mother," she wailed. "Sister Jerome says …" She became quite incoherent in a fresh paroxysm of tears.

"What does Sister Jerome say?" asked the Reverend Mother mildly.

Sister Jerome cleared her throat. "That mark, Mother. I think it's blood."

Sister Gertrude's knees felt quite wobbly. She gulped, "And we can't find Sister Anne anywhere."

CHAPTER TWO

Inspector C.D. Sloan had never been inside a Convent before.

He had, he reckoned, been inside most places of female confinement in his working life—hospitals, prisons, orphanages, offices, and even—once—a girls' boarding school. (That had been in pursuit of a Ward in Chancery whom a great many other people had been pursuing at the same time. Sloan had got there first, though it had been a near thing.)

But never so much as a monastery, let alone a Convent.

The call came into Berebury Police Station just before ten in the morning. The Criminal Investigation Department of the Berebury Division of the Calleshire Constabulary was not large, and as his sergeant was checking up on the overactivities of a bigamist, he had no choice at all about whom he took with him to the Convent: Crosby, Detective-Constable, William. Raw, perky, and consciously representing the younger generation in the force, he was one of those who provoked Superintendent Leeyes into observing (at least once every day) that these young constables weren't what they were.

"You'll do, I suppose," said Sloan resignedly. "Let's go." He stepped into the police car and Crosby drove the five and a half miles to Cullingoak village. He slowed down at the entrance to a gaunt red-brick building just outside Cullingoak proper and prepared to turn into the drive. Sloan looked up.

"Not here. Farther on."

Crosby changed gear. "Sorry, sir, I thought ..."

"That's the Agricultural Institute. Where young gentlemen learn to be farmers. Or young farmers learn to be gentlemen." He grunted. "I forget which. The Convent is the next turning on the right."

It wasn't exactly plain sailing when they did find the entrance.

There was a high, close-boarded fence running alongside the road and the Convent was invisible behind it. The double doors set in it were high and locked. Crosby rattled the handle unsuccessfully.

"Doesn't look as if they're expecting us."

"From what I've heard," said Sloan dryly, "they should be."

Eventually Crosby found his way in through a little door set in the big one.

"I'll open it from the inside for the car," he called over, but a minute or two later he reappeared baffled. "I can't, Inspector. There's some sort of complicated gadget here …"

"A mantrap?" suggested Sloan heavily.

"Could be. It won't open, anyway."

His superintendent didn't like his wit and his constables didn't appreciate it: which was, if anything, worse.

"Then we'll have to walk," he said.

"Walk?"

"Walk, Crosby. Like you did in the happy days of yore before they put you in the C.I.D. In fact, you can count yourself lucky you don't have to take your shoes off."

Crosby looked down at his regulation issues.

"Barefoot," amplified Sloan.

Crosby's brow cleared. "Like that chap in history who had to walk through the snow?"

"Henry Four."

"He'd upset somebody, hadn't he?"

"The Pope."

Crosby grinned at last. "I get you, sir. Pilgrimage or something, wasn't it?"

"Penance, actually."

Crosby didn't seem interested in the difference, and they plodded up the drive together between banks of rhododendrons. It wasn't wet, but an unpleasant early morning dampness dripped from the dank leaves. Nothing grew under the bushes. The drive twisted and turned, and at first they could see nothing but the bushes and trees.

Sloan glanced about him professionally. "Pretty well cared for really. Verges neat. No weeds. That box hedge over there was clipped properly."

"Slave labor," said Crosby, crunching along the drive beside him. "Don't these women have to do as they're told? Vow of obedience or something?" He kicked at a stone, sending it expertly between two bushes. "Anyone can get their gardening done that way."

"Anyone can tell you're still single, Crosby. Let me tell you that a vow of obedience won't get your gardening done for you. My wife promised to obey—got the vicar to leave it in the marriage service on purpose—but it doesn't signify. And," he added dispassionately, "if you think that shot would have got past the Calleford goalkeeper next Saturday afternoon, you're mistaken. He's got feet."

They rounded a bend and the Convent came into view, the drive opening out as they approached, finishing in a broad sweep in front of an imposing porch.

"Cor," said Crosby expressively.

"Nice, isn't it?" agreed Inspector Sloan. "Almost a young stately home, you might say. The Faine family used to live here and then one of them—the grandfather I suppose he would be—took to horses or it may have been cards. Something expensive anyway and they had to sell out." Sloan was a Calleshire man, born and bred. "The family's still around somewhere."

There were wide shallow steps in front of the porch, flanked by a pair of stone lions. And a large crest over the door.

Crosby spelled out the letters: "'*Pax Intrantibus, Salus Exeuntibus*'— that'll be the family motto, I suppose."

"More likely to be the good Sisters', Crosby. *Pax* means peace, and I don't think the Faines were a particularly peaceful lot in the old days."

"Yes, sir, but what about the rest of it?"

He wasn't catching Sloan out that easily.

"Look it up, constable," he said unfairly, "then you'll remember it better, won't you?"

"Yes, sir."

Sloan climbed the last step and advanced to the door.

"Sir …"

"Yes, Crosby?"

"Er, what gives?"

"Didn't you get the message?" Sloan pressed the bell. "Something nasty has happened to a nun."

Unexpectedly a little light flashed on at the side of the door. Crosby peered forward and read aloud the notice underneath it: "'Open the door and enter the hall.'"

"Advance and be recognized," interpreted Sloan, who had done his time in the Army.

They pushed open the outer door and stood inside a brightly- lit vestibule. The next pair of doors was of glass. There was another notice attached to these: "When the buzzer sounds push these doors." Beyond them was a small hall, and at the other side of this was a screen stretching from floor to ceiling. In the centre of the screen was a grille.

Sloan was suddenly aware of a face looking at them through it. The two policemen were standing in the light, and beyond the grille was shadow, so they could see little of the face except that it was there—watching them. The scrutiny ended with a buzzer sounding loudly—and the lock on the glass door fell open.

Sloan pushed the doors and walked forward into the hall.

The face behind the grille retreated a fraction into the dark background and he saw it no better.

Sloan cleared his throat. "I am Detective-Inspector Sloan from Berebury C.I.D."

"Yes?" The voice was uninviting.

"I understand that one of the nuns—"

"Sister Anne."

Behind his right ear he heard Crosby struggling to strangle a snort at birth.

"Sister Anne," continued Sloan hastily, "I am told has had … has unfortunately met with an …"

"She's dead," said the face.

"Just so," said Sloan, who was finding it downright disconcerting talking to someone he could not see.

"She's in the cellar," volunteered the speaker.

"That's what I had heard."

The voice attached to the face was Irish and that was about all Sloan could tell.

"I think you had better see the Mother Superior," she said.

"So do I," said Sloan.

There was a faint click and a shutter came down over the grille. The two policemen waited.

There were two doors leading out of the hall but both were locked. Crosby turned his attention to the lock on the glass doors.

"Electricity, sir. That's how it works."

"I didn't suppose it was magic," said Sloan irritably. "Did you?"

This wasn't the sort of delay he liked when there was a body about. Superintendent Leeyes wasn't going to like it either. He would be sitting in his office, waiting—and wondering why he hadn't heard from them already.

They went on waiting. The hall was quite silent. There were two chairs there and, on one wall, a little plaster Madonna with a red lamp burning before it. Nothing else. Crosby finished his prowling and came back to stand restively beside Sloan.

"At this rate, sir, it doesn't look as if they're going to let the dog get a look at the rabbit at all. …"

There was the mildest of deprecating coughs behind his right ear and Crosby spun round. Somewhere, somehow, a door must have opened and two nuns come through it, but neither policeman had heard it happen.

"Forgive us, gentlemen, if we startled you …"

Sloan had an impression of immense authority—something rare in a woman—and the calm that went with it. She was standing quite still, dignity incarnate, her hands folded loosely together in front of her black habit, her expression perfectly composed.

"Not at all," he said, discomfited.

"I am the Mother Superior. …"

"How do you do …" The conventional police "madam" hung unspoken, inappropriate, in the air. Sloan's own mother was a vigorous woman in her early seventies. He struggled to use the word and failed.

"… Marm," he finished, inspired.

"And this is Sister Mary St. Lucy."

That was easier. He could call the whole world "Sister."

"Sister Lucy is our Bursar and Procuratrix …"

Sloan saw Crosby's startled glance and shot him a look calculated to wither him into silence.

The Mother Superior glanced briefly round the hall. "I am sorry that Sister Porteress kept you waiting here. She should have shown you to the Parlor." She smiled faintly. "She interprets her watchdog duties very seriously. Besides which …" again the faint smile "… she has a rooted objection to policemen."

It was Sloan's experience that a lot of people had, but that they didn't usually say so straight out.

"Not shared, I hope, marm, by all your Sisters. …"

"I couldn't tell you, Inspector," she said simply. "This is the first time one has ever crossed our threshold." She turned to one of the doors. "I therefore know very little about your routine but I dare say you would like to see Sister Anne. ..."

"Not half," whispered Crosby to her back.

"And Sister Peter, too, though I fear she won't be of much immediate help to you. She's quite overcome, so I've sent her to the kitchen. They're always glad of an extra pair of hands there at this time of the day. This way, please."

She led them through the nearer of the two doors into what had been the original entrance hall of the old house. It was two stories high, with a short landing across one end. A pair of double doors led through into the chapel at the other end, but the center of attraction was the great carved black oak staircase. Its only carpet was polish, and it descended in a series of stately treads from the balustraded gallery at the top to a magnificent newel post at the bottom, elaborately carved, with an orb sitting on the top.

The Mother Superior did not spare it a glance but, closely followed by Sister Lucy, led them off behind the staircase through a dim corridor smelling of beeswax. Sloan followed, guided as much by the sound of the long rosaries which hung from their waists as by sight. Once they passed another nun coming the opposite way. Sloan tried to get a good look at her face, but when she saw the Reverend Mother and her party, she drew quietly to one side and stood, eyes cast down, until they had all passed. Then they heard the slight clink of her rosary as she walked on.

"Inspector," Crosby hissed in his ear, "they're all wearing wedding rings."

"Brides of Christ," Sloan hissed back.

"What's that?"

"I'll tell you later."

The Reverend Mother had halted in front of one of the several doors leading off the corridor.

"This is the way to the cellar, Inspector. Sister Anne, God rest her soul, is at the foot of the steps."

So she was.

Sister Lucy opened the door and Sloan saw a figure lying on the floor. Two nuns were kneeling beside it in an attitude of prayer. He went down the steps carefully. They were steep, and the lighting was not of the brightest.

When they saw the new arrivals, the two nuns who had been keeping vigil by the body rose quietly and melted into the background.

The body of the nun was spread-eagled on the stone floor, face downwards, her habit caught up, her veil knocked askew. The white bloodless hands were all he could see of death at first. There was a plain broad silver ring on the third finger of this left hand too.

The Reverend Mother and Sister Lucy crossed themselves and then drew back a little, watching him.

He couldn't tell in the bad light where the blood on her black habit began and ended, but there was no doubt from where it had come. The back of her head. Even in this light he could see there was something wrong with its shape. There was a hollow where no hollow should be.

He knelt beside her and bent to see her face. There was blood there, too, but he couldn't see any. . . .

"We would have liked to have moved her," said the Reverend Mother, "or at least have covered her up, but Dr. Carret said on no account to touch anything until you came."

"Quite right," he said absently. "Crosby, have you a torch there?"

He shone it on the dead Sister's face. Blood from the back of her skull had trickled forward round the sides of the white linen cloth she wore under her cowl and round her head and cheeks. There was a word for it that he had heard somewhere once ... w ... w ... wimple ... that was it. Well, her wimple had held a lot of the blood back, but quite a bit had got through to run down her face and then—surely—to drip on the floor. Only that was the funny thing. It hadn't reached the floor. He swept the beam from the torch on it again. There was no blood on the floor. That on the face was congealed and dry, but there was enough of it for some to have dripped down on the floor.

And it hadn't.

"So, of course, we didn't touch anything until you saw her." The quiet voice of the Reverend Mother obtruded into his thoughts. "But now that you have seen her, will it be all right for us to ..."

"No," said Sloan heavily. "It won't be all right for you to do anything at all." He got to his feet again. "I want a police photographer down here first, and any moving that's to be done will be done by the police surgeon's men."

"Perhaps then Sister Lucy might just have her keys back, Inspector?"

"Keys?"

Sister Lucy flushed. "I lent them to poor Sister Anne late yesterday afternoon. She was going to go through our store cupboards to make up some parcels for Christmas. We have Sisters in the mission field, you know, and they are very glad of things for their people at this time. She did it every year." She hesitated. "You can just see the edges of them under her habit there. …"

"No."

"You must forgive us," interposed the Mother Superior gently. "We are sometimes a little out of touch here with civil procedure, and we have never had a fatal accident here before. We have no wish to transgress any law."

He stared at her. "It isn't a question of the infringement of any rule, marm. It is simply that I am not satisfied that I know exactly how Sister Anne died. Moreover, you also have a nun here with blood on her hands which you say she is unable to explain …"

"Just," apologetically, "on one thumb."

"And," continued Sloan majestically, "you want me to allow you to move a body and remove from it evidence which may or may not be material. No, marm, I'm afraid the keys will have to wait until the police surgeon has been. Have you a telephone here?"

The Mother Superior smiled her faint smile. "In that sense at least, Inspector, we are in touch with the world."

CHAPTER THREE

"Wait a minute, wait a minute," grumbled Sister Polycarp. "I'm coming as fast as I can." She stumped towards the front door. "Ringing the bell like that! It's enough to waken the dead." She stopped abruptly. "No, it's not, you know. It won't wake poor Sister Anne, not now." She drew the grille back. "Oh, it's you, Father. Come in. They're waiting for you in the Parlor. It's about poor Sister Anne. She, poor soul, has gone to her reward and we've got the police here."

"A nice juxtaposition of clauses," said Father MacAuley.

"What's that?"

"Nothing, Sister, nothing." Father MacAuley stepped inside. "Just an observation. ..."

"Oh, I see. I should have kept them out myself, but Mother said that wouldn't help. Can't abide the police."

"You're prejudiced, Polycarp. Nobody worries about the Troubles any more. You won't believe this but the Irish Question is no longer a burning matter of moment. You're out of touch."

Sister Polycarp sniffed again. "That's as may be. You're too young to remember, Father. But I never thought to have the police trampling about again, that I can tell you. Arrest poor Sister Peter, that's what they'll do."

"Will they indeed?" Father MacAuley looked thoughtfully at the nun. "That's the little one that squeaks when you speak to her, isn't it? Now why should they arrest her?"

"Oh, you know what they're like. She's got some blood on her hand and she doesn't know how it got there."

"Tiresome," agreed Father MacAuley.

"Otherwise it would have been a straightforward fall down the cellar steps and that would have been an end to it. Unfortunate of course"—Sister Polycarp recollected that not only was she speaking about the dead, but the newly dead, and crossed herself—"but we could have sent the police packing. As it is they look like being underfoot for a long time."

"Do they now?" Father MacAuley took off his coat. "In that case …"

"It wouldn't matter so much," burst out Sister Polycarp, "if everyone didn't know."

Father MacAuley wagged a reproving finger. "Polycarp, I do believe that you're worried about what the neighbors will think."

She bridled. "It's not very nice, now, is it, for people to be seeing the police at a Convent?"

Where a lesser woman might have bustled into the Parlor, the Reverend Mother contrived to arrive there ahead of her own habit, rosary and rather breathless attendant Sister Lucy.

"Father—thank you for coming so quickly. Poor Sister Anne's lying dead at the bottom of the cellar steps and we do seem to be in a rather delicate position. …"

"Sister Peter want bailing out?"

"Not yet, thank you. No, I fancy it's not the presence of blood on the Gradual so much as the absence of blood elsewhere that's going to be the trouble. Don't you agree, Sister?"

Sister Lucy nodded intelligently. "Yes, Mother."

Father MacAuley sat down. "Sister Anne, now she was the one with the glasses, wasn't she?"

"That's right," agreed Sister Lucy. "She couldn't see without them. Missions were her great interest, you know."

He frowned. "Fairly tall?"

"About my height, I suppose," said Sister Lucy.

"But older?"

"That's right. She was professed before I joined the Order. Perhaps Mother can tell you when that would have been. …"

"No, no, I can't offhand. But I do know how she would have hated having been the cause of all this trouble. She wasn't a fusser, you know. In fact," she paused, "she wasn't the sort of Sister whom anything happened to at all."

"Until now," pointed out Father MacAuley.

"Until now," agreed the Mother Superior somberly.

There was a light tap on the Parlor door. Sister Lucy opened it to a very young nun.

"Please, Mother, Sister Cellarer says if she can't get into any of the store cupboards we'll have to have parkin for afters because she made that yesterday."

"Thank you, Sister, and say to Sister Cellarer that that will be very nice, thank you." The door shut after the nun and the Reverend Mother turned to Sister Lucy. "What is parkin?"

"A North Country gingerbread dish, Mother."

"Eaten especially on Guy Fawkes' Night," added MacAuley. "A clear instance, if I may say so, of tradition overtaking theology."

"It often does," observed the Mother Prioress placidly, "but this is not the moment to go into that with a cook who can't get to her food cupboards." She told him about the keys. "However, Inspector Sloan is telephoning his headquarters now. Perhaps after that we shall be allowed to have them back."

The Convent keys did not, in fact, figure in the conversation Inspector Sloan had with his superior.

"Speak up, Sloan, I can't hear you."

"Sorry, sir, I'm speaking from the Convent. The telephone here is a bit public."

There was a grunt at the other end of the line. "Like that, is it? Devil of a long time you've been coming through. What happened?"

"This nun is dead all right. Has been for quite a few hours, I should say. The body's cold, though the cellar's pretty perishing anyway and that may not be much to go on. I'd like a few photographs and Dr. Dabbe, too. ..."

"The whole box of tricks?"

"Yes, please, sir—she's lying at the foot of a flight of stairs with a nasty hole in the back of her head."

"All right, Sloan, I'll buy it. Did she fall or was she pushed?"

"That's the interesting thing, Superintendent. I don't think it was either."

"Not like the moon and green cheese?"

"I beg your pardon, sir?"

"Either it is made of green cheese or it isn't."

"N—no, sir, I don't think so."

"If it's not one of the two possible alternatives then it must be the other, always provided, of course, that ..."

Sloan sighed. Superintendent Leeyes had started going to an Adult
Education Class on Logic this autumn and it was playing havoc with his
powers of reasoning.

"I've left Crosby down in the cellar with the body, sir, until Dr. Dabbe
gets here."

"All right, Sloan, I know when I'm being deflected. But remember—
failure to carry a line of thought through to its logical conclusion means
confusion."

"Yes, sir."

"Now, what was this woman called?"

"Sister Anne," said Sloan cautiously.

"Ha!" The superintendent ran true to form. "Perhaps she *didn't* see
anyone coming, eh?"

"No, sir."

"And her real name?"

"I don't know yet. The Reverend Mother has gone to look it up."

"Right. Keep me informed. By the way, Sloan, who found her in the
cellar?"

"I was afraid you were going to ask me that, sir."

"Why?"

"You're not going to like it, sir."

"No?"

"No, sir." Unhappily. "It was Sister St. Bernard."

The telephone gave an angry snarl. "I don't like it, Sloan. If I find
you've been taking the micky, there's going to be trouble, understand?"

"Yes, sir."

"And Sloan …"

"Sir?"

"If you expect that to go in the official report, you had better bring that
little barrel of brandy back with you."

Sloan waited for Dr. Dabbe at the top of the cellar steps and wished on
the whole that he was back at the girls' boarding school. He could understand their rules. Not long afterwards the police surgeon appeared in the
dim corridor, ushered along by a new Sister.

"Morning, Sloan. Something for me, I understand, in the cellar."

"A nun, doctor. At the bottom of this flight of stairs."

"Aha," said Dr. Dabbe alertly. "And she hasn't been moved?"

"Not by us," said Sloan.

"Like that, is it? Right."

Sloan opened the door inwards, disclosing a scene that, but for the stolid Crosby, could have come—almost—from an artist's illustration for an historical novel. The two attendant Sisters were still there, kneeling, and the dead Sister lying on the floor. The solitary, unshaded electric light reflected their shadows grotesquely against the whitewashed walls.

"Quite medieval," observed Dabbe. "Shall we look at the steps as we go down?"

"There's not a lot to see," said Sloan. "Several of the nuns and the local G.P., Dr. Carret, went up and down before we got here, but there is one mark at the side of the seventh step that could be from her foot, and there is some dust on the right shoe that could be from the step. On the top of the shoe."

"Just so," agreed Dabbe, following the direction of the beam from Sloan's torch. "Steps dusted recently but not very recently."

The Sister with them coughed. "Probably about once a week, doctor."

"Thank you." He glanced from the step to the body. "Head first, Sloan, would you say?"

"Perhaps."

"I see." The pathologist reached the bottom step, nodded to Crosby, bowed gravely in the direction of the two kneeling nuns and turned his attention to the body. He looked at it for a long time from several angles and then said conversationally, "Interesting."

"Yes," said Sloan.

"Plenty of blood."

"Yes."

"Except in the one place where you'd expect it."

Sloan nodded obliquely. "The photograph boys are on their way."

"I know," Dabbe said blandly. "I overtook them." The pathologist was reckoned to be the fastest driver in Calleshire. "Notwithstanding any pretty pictures they may take, you can take it from me that whatever this woman died from, she didn't die in the spot where she is now lying."

"That," said Sloan, "is what I thought."

If anything Sloan appeared relieved to see another man in the Parlor.

"Our priest, Inspector—Father Benedict MacAuley." The Reverend Mother's rosary clinked as she moved forward. "I asked him to come here as I felt in need of some assistance in dealing with—er—external matters. Do you mind if he is present?"

"Not at all, marm. I have left the police surgeon in the cellar. In the meantime, perhaps you would tell us a little about the ... Sister Anne."

Sloan wouldn't have chosen the Convent Parlor for an interview with anyone. It was the reverse of cozy. The Reverend Mother and Sister Lucy disposed themselves on hard, stiff-backed chairs and offered two others to the two policemen. Father MacAuley was settled in the only one that looked remotely comfortable. Sloan noticed that it was the policemen who were in the light, the Reverend Mother who was in the shadow, from the window. Vague thoughts about the Inquisition flitted through his mind and were gone again. The room was bare, as the entrance hall had been bare, the floor of highly polished wood. In most rooms there was enough to give a good policeman an idea of the type of person he was interviewing—age, sex, standards, status. Here there was nothing at all. The overriding impression was still beeswax.

The Reverend Mother folded her hands together in her lap and said quietly, "The name of Sister Anne was Josephine Mary Cartwright. That is all that I can tell you about her life before she came to the Convent. We have a Mother House, you understand, in London, and our records are kept there. I would have to telephone there, for her last address and date of profession. I'm sorry—that seems very little ..."

Sister Lucy lifted her head slightly and said to the Reverend Mother: "She was English."

"As opposed to what?" asked Sloan quickly.

"Irish or French."

"Frequently opposed to both," said the Reverend Mother unexpectedly. "When all else is submerged, that sort of nationality remains. It is a curious feature of Convent life."

"Indeed? Now we had a message this morning ..."

"That would be from Dr. Carret. He is so kind to us always. We sent for him at once."

"When would that have been, marm?"

"After Office this morning. We didn't know about last night."

"What about last night?"

"That she might have been lying there since then."

"What makes you think that?"

"Dr. Carret, Inspector. He said that was what had probably happened."

"I see. But you didn't miss her?"

"Not until this morning."

"When?"

"The Caller, Sister Gertrude, found her cell empty this morning. She thought first of all that she had merely risen early, but as she was not at breakfast either she mentioned it to the Infirmarium."

"Then what happened?"

"After Office the Sister Infirmarium went to her cell to see if she was unwell."

"And?"

"She reported to me that her cell was empty."

"Had her bed been slept in?"

"I do not think Sister Infirmarium would have been in a position to know that. All the beds are made by the Sisters themselves ..."

"It might have been warm." Sloan shifted his weight on the hard chair. "You can usually tell with your hand even if the bed has been aired—especially in winter."

The Mother Superior's manner stiffened perceptibly. "I do not suppose such a procedure occurred to Sister Infirmarium."

"Of course not," appeased Sloan hastily. Did he imagine the priest's sympathetic glance? For all he knew "bed" might be a taboo word in this Convent—in any Convent. Probably was. He took refuge in a formula. "I should like to see Sister Inf ... Infirmarium presently. And this Sister Peter."

"Ah, yes, Sister Peter." The Reverend Mother's eyes rested reflectively on the inspector. "The blood seems to have appeared on her thumb before Mass, and some of it was transferred to the Gradual during the service. ..."

"You left it?" interrupted Sloan.

"Yes, Inspector," she said gently, "we left it for you."

"What did you do when you were told about the blood and that Sister Anne was missing?"

"I asked Sister Lucy here to help look for her."

"Just Sister Lucy?"

"At first. A Convent is a busy place, Inspector."

"Yes, marm, I'm sure"—untruthfully.

"When their search failed to reveal her in any of the places where she might have been expected to have been taken ill, I asked other Sisters to go over the house and grounds very carefully."

"I see."

"This is a big house and it took some time, but, as you know, Sister St. Bernard opened the cellar door and put the light on ... you will want to see her, too, I take it?"

"Yes, please, marm."

"We telephoned Dr. Carret and he came at once. It was he who was so insistent on our leaving her lying on that cold floor."

"Very right, marm." He answered the unspoken reproach as best he could. "I'm afraid this will be a police matter until we find out exactly what happened. Tell me, marm, at what time would everyone have gone to bed last night?"

At the boarding school it had been "lights out."

"Nine o'clock."

"And after that no one would have gone into anyone else's bedroom. ..."

"No one is allowed in anyone else's cell at any time except the Caller, who is Sister Gertrude, the Infirmarium and myself."

"I see. Presumably no one checks that the Sisters are in their cells?"

"No."

This was not, after all, a boarding school.

"I am seeking, marm, to establish when Sister Anne was last seen alive."

"At Vespers at half past eight."

"By whom?"

"Sister Michael and Sister Damien. Their stalls are on either side of Sister Anne's."

"And you can tell me of nothing that might have caused Sister Anne to leave her cell last night?"

"Nothing. In fact, it is forbidden."

That, decided Sloan, settled that. For the time being.

"I see, marm, thank you." He stood up. "Now, if you would be so kind as to get in touch with your—er—head office ..."

"Inspector ..."

"Yes, marm?" Sloan was ready with a handful of routine phrases about inquests, postmortems and the like.

The Mother Prioress's rosary clinked. "It is one of the privileges of Convent life that strangers do not perform the Last Office. We always do that for our own Sisters ourselves."

It was something that he had never considered.

CHAPTER FOUR

The cellar was quite crowded by the time Sloan and Crosby got back there. Two police photographers had joined the unmerry throng and were heaving heavy cameras about. Dr. Dabbe was still contemplating the body from all angles. The two Sisters were still praying—and the photographers didn't like it.

"Hey, Inspector," whispered one of them. "Call your dogs off, can't you? Giving us the creeps kneeling there. And getting in the way. I want some pictures from over that side but I'm blowed if I'm going on my knees beside them."

"It might give them the wrong idea, Dyson," agreed Sloan softly. "They don't know you as well as I do." He glanced across the cellar. "They're not upsetting the doctor."

"He's a born exhibitionist. All pathologists are and nothing upsets him. Nothing at all. I sometimes wonder if he's human." Dyson screwed a new flash bulb into its socket. "Besides, I don't want those two figuring in any pix I do take. Or I'll be spending the rest of my life explaining that they're not ravens from the Tower of London or the Ku Klux Klan or something."

"Too much imagination, Dyson, that's your trouble."

Nevertheless, he went back upstairs and found Sister Lucy.

"Certainly, Inspector," she said, when he explained. "I will ask the Sisters to continue their prayers and vigil in the Chapel."

Sloan murmured that that would do very nicely, thank you.

At a word from her the two Sisters in the cellar rose from their knees in one economical movement, crossed themselves and withdrew.

"That's better," said Dyson, changing plates rapidly. "It's our artistic temperaments, you know, Inspector. Very sensitive to atmosphere."

"Get on with it," growled Sloan.

Dyson jerked a finger at his assistant and crouched on his knees in a manner surprisingly reminiscent of that of the two nuns. Instead of having his hands clasped in front of him they held a heavy camera. He pressed a button and, for a moment, the whole cellar became illumined in a harsh, bright light.

A moment later the pathologist came up to him.

"I don't know about Mr. Fox over there," said Dr. Dabbe, "but I've finished down here for the time being. I've got the temperature readings—did you notice she was in a draught, by the way?—and all I need about the position of the body. It's cold down here but not damp. At the moment I can't tell you much more than Carret—a good chap, incidentally—that she died yesterday evening sometime. The body is quite cold. You'll have to wait for more exact details—which is a pity because I dare say it's important ..."

"Yes," said Sloan.

"I'll be as quick as I can." He paused. "From what I can see from here there's a fair bit of post-mortem injury—I think she was dead before she was put in this cellar and then damaged by the fall and so forth."

"Nice," said Sloan shortly.

"Very," agreed the pathologist. "Especially here."

"Cause of death?"

"Depressed fracture of skull."

"Can I quote you?"

"Lord, yes. I don't need her on the table for that. You can see it from here. That's not to say she hasn't other injuries as well, but that'll do for a start, won't it?"

Sloan nodded gloomily.

Dabbe picked up his hat. "I've got a sample of the dust from that step and the shoe—I can tell you a bit more about that later. And the time of death. ..."

The quiet of the cellar was shattered suddenly by a bell ringing. No sooner had it stopped than they could hear the reverberations of many feet moving about above them.

"In some ways," observed Sloan sententiously, "this place has much in common with a girls' boarding school."

"You don't say?" Dabbe cast a long, raking glance over the body on the floor. "Of course, I don't get about as much as you chaps. ... What's the bell for? Physical jerks?"

"Meditation."

"They could start on one or two little matters down here. I shall give my attention to a thumbprint on a manuscript, and I'll get my chap to begin on the blood grouping."

Sloan saw him out and then came back to the cellar. "Dyson ..."

"Inspector?"

"The name of your assistant?"

"Williams."

"I thought so. Who is Mr. Fox?"

Dyson hitched his camera over his shoulder and prepared to depart. "One of the inventors of photography, blast him."

The cellar door banged behind the two photographers, leaving Sloan and Crosby alone with Sister Anne at last.

"Now, then, Crosby, where are we?"

Crosby pulled out his notebook. "We have one female body—of a nun—said to be Sister Anne alias Josephine ..."

"Not alias, Crosby."

"Maiden name of—no, that doesn't sound right either. They're all maidens, aren't they?"

"So I understand."

"Well, then ..."

"Secular."

"Oh, really? Secular name of Josephine Mary Cartwright. Medium to tall in height, age uncertain ..."

"Unknown."

"Unknown, suffering from a fractured skull ..."

"At least ..."

"At least—sustained we know not how but somewhere else."

"Not well put but I am with you."

"As I see it, sir, that's the lot."

"See again, Crosby, because it isn't."

"No?" Crosby looked injured.

"No," said Sloan.

They waited in the cellar until two men appeared with a stretcher and then gave them a hand with the ticklish job of getting their burden up the stairs. Then ...

"Inspector, I've been thinking ..."

"Good. I thought you would get there in the end."

"If that was the top of her shoe that hit the seventh step, then she didn't even die somewhere else in the cellar."

"Granted."

"Someone threw her down those steps after she was dead?"

"That's what Dr. Dabbe thinks."

"That's a nasty way to carry on in a Convent."

"Barbarous," agreed Sloan, and waited.

Crosby, untrammeled by classes on Logic, should be able to get further than that on his own.

"The fall didn't kill her?" he suggested tentatively.

"Not this fall anyway." He looked at the steep stairs. "A weapon more like."

"A weapon seems sort of out of place here."

"So does a body in a cellar," said Sloan crisply. "Especially one that didn't die there."

Crosby took that point too. "You mean," he said slowly, "that they parked her somewhere else before they chucked her down?"

"I do. For how long?"

He was quicker this time. "For long enough for the blood on her head to dry because it didn't drip on the floor?"

"You're doing nicely, Crosby."

Crosby grinned. "So we look for somewhere where someone stashed away a bleeding nun and/or whatever it was they hit her with?"

"If we have to tear the place apart," agreed Sloan gravely.

In the event they didn't.

Prowling about in the dim corridor at the top of the cellar steps was Father MacAuley. He was on his hands and knees when Sloan almost fell over him.

"Ah, Inspector," he said unnecessarily, "there you are."

"Yes, sir, and there you are, too, so to speak." He regarded the kneeling figure expressionlessly. "If it will save you any trouble, sir, I have already ascertained that this corridor was swept and polished early this morning."

"Really?" He got to his feet. "Good. Then we can get on with the next thing, can't we?"

"What's that, sir?"

"Finding where they left her until they pushed her down the steps, of course. It must be off this corridor somewhere."

"Why is that, sir?"

"Too risky to drag a body across that enormous hall, don't you think? Someone might have come out of the Chapel at any moment and there's that gallery at the top of the stairs. Anyone might be watching from there. No, I think she was—er—done to death round about here, or perhaps through in the kitchens somewhere."

"We'll see, sir, shall we?"

Sloan opened the nearest door, but the priest shook his head.

"No, Inspector, it won't be there. That's the—er—necessarium. It's hardly big enough. Besides, the door only locks on the inside and there would always be the risk of someone wanting to use it, wouldn't there?"

The second and third doors revealed a small library, and a garden room with outside glass door, sink and vases.

They found what they were looking for behind the fourth door. It opened on to a large broom cupboard. Crosby's torch played over the brown stain on the bare boards of the cupboard's floor.

MacAuley peered inquisitively over their shoulders. "Someone kept their head—looks as if she was put in here head first so that the blood was as far away from the door as possible."

Crosby shifted the angle of the torch's beam and said, "Those nuns have been in here this morning for these brooms, I'll be bound."

Sloan sniffed the polish in the air. "I dare say. They wouldn't have noticed this blood though, not without a light. We'll see if the doctor has left."

"Constable, if I might just borrow your torch. ..." MacAuley took it deftly from Crosby and began to cover the broom cupboard inch by inch in its beam.

Crosby stepped back into the corridor.

"Inspector ..."

"Well?"

"What did whoever put her in here want to go and move her for?"

"Take a bit longer to find perhaps."

"Would that matter?"

"I don't know yet, but even the most absentminded of this crew would have noticed her when they came to do the cleaning this morning."

Sloan was keeping a close eye on Father Benedict MacAuley withal. "Besides, you do get a broken skull sometimes from falling down the cellar steps but very rarely from tripping over in a broom cupboard."

"They hoped we would think she had fallen down those nasty steep stairs?"

"I shouldn't be at all surprised. Most people expect the police to jump to the wrong conclusions. And if you never do, Crosby, you will end up ..." He paused. Father MacAuley was backing out of the cupboard.

"Where, Inspector?" Crosby was ambitious.

Sloan looked at him. "Exactly where you are now—as a Detective-Constable with the Berebury C.I.D.—because you wouldn't be human enough for promotion. Well, Father MacAuley, have you found what you were looking for?"

"No, I can't think what has happened to them."

"Happened to what?" asked Sloan patiently.

"Sister Anne's glasses. She couldn't see without them, and yet they're nowhere to be found."

CHAPTER FIVE

Considering how little of the flesh of a nun could be seen, Sloan marveled how much he was aware of the differing personalities of the Mother Prioress and Sister Lucy. In both cases good bone structure stood out beneath the tight white band across the forehead. There was self-control, too, in the line of both mouths, and, in Sister Lucy's case, more than a little beauty still. She must have been very good-looking indeed once, and that not so very long ago.

He opened his notebook. "Now, marm, with regard to comings and goings, so to speak—exactly how private are you here?"

That would be the first thing Superintendent Leeyes would want to know—an "inside" job or an "outside" one. On this hung a great many things.

"We are not a strictly enclosed Order, Inspector. Sisters are allowed to leave the Convent for works of necessity and mercy, and so forth. They have interviews here in the Parlor unless it is a Clothing, when they come into the Chapel. Our Chapel was originally the Faine private one, and Mrs. Faine and her daughter still attend services here, as do others in Cullingoak." She smiled gently. "We are, in fact, to have a rather special service here next month. Miss Faine is to be married to Mr. Ranby, the Institute's Principal, and the Bishop has given his consent to our Chapel being used—as it would have been had the Faines still lived here."

"How do they get in?" enquired Sloan with interest.

"There is a door leading outside from the Chapel. Sister Polycarp unlocks it before the service."

"Tradesmen?"

"We have everything delivered. Sister Cellarer deals with them at the back door, and Sister Lucy here pays them."

"No one else?"

"Just Hobbett—he's our handyman. There are some tasks—just one or two, you understand—which are beyond our capacities."

Sloan nodded. "This Hobbett—does he have to run the gauntlet every day?"

"Past Sister Polycarp? No, his work is at the back. He has his own key to the boiler room and his own routine—dustbins, ladders, cleaning the upstairs outside windows and so forth. And the boiler for three-quarters of the time."

"Three quarters?"

"Sister Ignatius is the only person who can persuade it to function at all when the wind is in the east. Her devotions are frequently interrupted."

They found Hobbett in a small, not uncozy room at the foot of a short flight of outside stairs descending to cellar level not far from the kitchen door. It was lined with logs, and a litter of broken pieces of wood covered the floor. There was a chair with one arm broken and an old table. Hobbett was sitting at this having his midday break. There was a mug of steaming tea on the table. He was reading a popular daily newspaper with a tradition of the sensational.

"I am Inspector Sloan."

The man took a noisy sip of tea and set the mug down carefully on the table. "Hobbett."

He hadn't shaved this morning.

"We are enquiring into the death of Sister Anne."

Hobbett took another sip of tea. "I heard one of 'em had fallen down the cellar steps." He jerked his head towards the door in the corner. "I don't go through that far meself or happen I might 'ave found her for you."

"How far do you go through?"

"Just to the boiler—got to keep that going—and the coke place with kindling and that. Mostly I work in the grounds."

To Sloan he hadn't the look of a man who worked anywhere.

"What were you doing yesterday?"

"Yesterday?" Hobbett looked surprised. "I'd 'ave to think." He took a long pull at his tea. "I cleared out a drain first. The gutter from the Chapel roof was blocked with leaves and I had to get my ladders out. Long job, that was. I'd just finished when Sister Lucy sent for me to shift a window that'd got stuck."

"Upstairs or down?"

"Up. I'd just put my ladders away, too. She wouldn't have it left though. Said it was dangerous. One of 'em might have escaped through it, I suppose." He drank the rest of his tea in one long swallow and licked his lips. "Not that there's much for them to escape for, is there now?"

"This Sister Anne," said Sloan sharply. "Did you see her often?"

"Wouldn't know her if I did. Can't tell some of them from which, if you get me. There's about four of them that gives me orders. The rest don't bother me much."

"When did you leave last night?"

"Short of five somewhere. Can't do much in the dark."

"Nice type," observed Crosby on their way back.

"And four doors," said Sloan morosely, "and about thirty windows."

Sister Gertrude was having a bad day. First, though no one had mentioned it, she was deeply conscious of her neglect in ignoring Sister Anne's empty cell. And now she was troubled about something else. As a nervous postulant she had fondly imagined that there would be no worries in a Convent, that the way would be clear and that obedience to the Rule would make following that way, if not easy, then at least straightforward.

It seemed she was wrong—or was she?

No nun was meant to carry worries that properly belonged to the Reverend Mother. Her instructions were simple. The Reverend Mother was to be told of them and her ruling was absolute. Then the Sister concerned need worry no longer.

What they had omitted to pontificate on, thought Sister Gertrude, was at what point a worry became substantial enough for communicating to the Reverend Mother. What was bothering her was just an uneasy thought.

It had cropped up after luncheon. There was no proper recreation until the early evening, but after their meal there was a brief relaxation of the silence in which they worked. It lasted for about fifteen minutes until they resumed their duties for the afternoon. And the person who had been speaking to her in it was Sister Damien.

In the tradition of the Convent an empty place was left at the refectory table where Sister Anne had always sat, her napkin laid alongside it. It would be so for seven days and then the ranks of nuns would close up as if she had never been. And Sister Damien and Sister Michael who had sat for several years on either side of Sister Anne would now for the rest of their mortal lives sit next to each other instead at meals, in Chapel, and in everything else they did as a Community.

"I think we will have our cloister now," Sister Damien had remarked as they tidied up the refectory together.

"Our cloister? Now?" Sister Gertrude stopped and looked at her. The Convent had always lacked a cloister but to build one as they would have liked by joining up two back wings of the house was well beyond their means. "We shall need one very badly if they build next door, but where will the money come from?"

Sister Damien assiduously chased a few wayward crumbs along one of the tables. "Sister Anne."

"Sister Anne?"

Sister Damien pinned down another crumb with her thin hand. "She knew we wanted a cloister."

"We all knew we wanted a cloister," said Sister Gertrude with some asperity. "It's very difficult in winter without one, but that doesn't mean to say that …"

"Sister Anne was to come into some money and she's left it to us."

"How do you know?"

"She told me," said Sister Damien simply. "She didn't have a dowry but she knew she was going to have this money some day."

Sister Gertrude pursed her lips. Money was never mentioned in the ownership sense in the Convent. In calculating wants and needs and ways and means, yes, but never relating to a particular Sister. And the size of a dowry was a matter between the Mother Superior and the Novice.

"So we'll be able to have our cloister now and it won't matter about the building," went on Sister Damien, oblivious of the effect she was creating. "That's good, isn't it?"

Sister Gertrude busied herself straightening a chair. "Yes," she said in as neutral a voice as she could manage. "Except for Sister Anne."

Sister Damien wheeled round and caught her arm. "But she is in Heaven, Sister. You don't regret that, do you?"

But Sister Gertrude did not know what it was she regretted, and at the first sound of the Convent bell she thankfully fled the refectory.

It was unfortunate for her peace of mind that the first person she bumped into was little Sister Peter. She was walking up the great staircase looking rather less cheerful than Mary Queen of Scots mounting the scaffold at Fotheringhay. She was holding her hand out in front of her with her thumb stuck out in odd disassociation from the rest of her body.

"Hasn't the Inspector finished with your thumb, Sister?" Sister Gertrude asked.

"Oh, yes," she said mournfully. "He's fingerprinted my hand, and confirmed that the blood did get on the Gradual from my thumb."

"Well, then," said Sister Gertrude a little testily, "surely you can put it away now?"

Sister Peter regarded the offending member. "He doesn't know how the blood got on it and neither do I. I've shown him everything I did this morning after you woke me—my own door, two flights of stairs to the long landing, the gallery, this staircase and straight into the Chapel. The Chapel door was open, Sister Polycarp does that. Sister Sacrist had got the Gradual ready like she always does. Besides everywhere's been cleaned by now. I just don't know ..." This last was said *tremolo*.

"Neither do I," said Sister Gertrude firmly. "But you've helped all you can. ..."

"I can't think why anyone should want to harm poor Sister Anne."

"Neither can I," said Sister Gertrude somewhat less firmly. "It might have been an accident, you know. ..."

Sister Peter looked unconvinced and continued on her way.

"Now, Sister St. Bernard, I realize that this business must have given you an unpleasant shock, but I would like you to describe how you found Sister Anne."

Sloan was back in the Parlor with Crosby in attendance facing the Reverend Mother with Sister Lucy at her side. Sister St. Bernard was standing between them. There would come a time when he would want to see a nun on her own but that time was not yet. Sister Lucy looked anxious and strained, but the Reverend Mother sat calm and dignified, an air of timelessness about her.

Sloan was being the perfect policeman talking to the nervous witness. There was no doubt that Sister St. Bernard was nervous. Her damp palms trembled slightly until she hit on the idea of clasping them together in front of her, but she could not keep a faint quaver out of her voice so easily.

"We were asked to help look for Sister Anne about an hour after Mass this morning in case she had been taken ill anywhere. Sister Lucy and the others were going through the upstairs rooms and Sister Perpetua and I were doing the downstairs ones. ..."

Sloan was prepared to bet that Sister Perpetua was as young as Sister St. Bernard and that no one had expected either of them to find the missing Sister.

"I don't know what made me open the cellar door. ... I had been in all the rooms along that corridor and—"

"Was it closed?"

"Yes."

"Properly?"

"Yes."

"Was it locked?"

"No."

"Are you sure about that?"

"Oh, yes. It was because it was usually locked that I put the light on when I opened it. Otherwise I don't think I would have seen Sister Anne."

"The door is normally kept locked, Inspector," explained the Reverend Mother in a very dry voice, "on account of the danger of falling down the steep steps in the dark."

"I see, marm, thank you. Then what did you do, Sister?"

She had done very little, decided Sloan, except give the alarm and encourage the destruction of useful clues by opening and shutting the cellar door and fetching people who went up and down the steps.

And Sister Peter had been scarcely more helpful.

When she had gone the Reverend Mother beckoned Sister Lucy to her side. "What was that address?"

"Seventeen Strelitz Square, Mother."

The Mother Prioress nodded. "Inspector, that was the address from which Sister Anne came to us."

"It's a very good one," said Sloan involuntarily.

"She was a very good nun," retorted the Reverend Mother dryly. "It was, of course, some time ago that she left home, but in the normal course of events I would telephone there to establish whether or not she still had relatives."

Sloan took a quick look at his watch. "Perhaps I'll telephone myself, marm."

Standing in the dark corridor where the nuns kept their instrument he wondered if it wouldn't have been wiser to go to London. When he was connected to 17 Strelitz Square he was sure.

"Mrs. Alfred Cartwright's residence," said a female voice.

"May I speak to Mrs. Cartwright, please?"

"Who shall I say is calling?"

"The Convent of St. Anselm." That would do to begin with.

"I will enquire if madam is at home."

There was a pause. Sloan heard footsteps walking away. Parquet flooring. And then they came back.

"Madam," said the female voice, "is Not At Home."

"It's about her daughter," said Sloan easily. "I think if she knew that she—"

"Madam has no daughter," said the voice and rang off.

Sloan went back to the Parlor. Only Crosby was there now.

"A bell rang, Inspector, and they both went—just like that. I didn't know if you wanted me to stop them."

"You? Stop them?" said Sloan unkindly. "You couldn't do it. Now, listen …"

There was a knock on the Parlor door and Father MacAuley came in.

"Ah, Inspector, found the glasses?"

"Not yet, sir," said Sloan shortly. It was bad enough investigating a death in the alien surroundings of a Convent without having a priest pattering along behind him. And MacAuley wasn't the only one who wanted to know where Sister Anne's glasses were. Superintendent Leeyes would be on to their absence in a flash, and a fat lot of good it would be explaining to him that he and Crosby had looked everywhere for them.

"Did you get anything out of Lady Macbeth?" asked the priest.

"We confirmed all of Sister Peter's statements," said Sloan stiffly.

"She's walking up and down the corridor muttering 'What! Will these hands ne'er be clean?' " He squinted at Sloan. "All the perfumes of Arabia will not sweeten that little hand."

"No, sir? The Mother Prioress tried an old Army remedy."

"She did?"

"Spud bashing."

"A fine leader of women, the Mother Prioress." Father MacAuley grinned suddenly. "I hear that the chap across the way—Ranby at the Agricultural Institute—he's gated his students for the evening. All to be in their own grounds by four o'clock this afternoon."

"Can't say I blame him for that," said Sloan. "Last year they burnt down the bus shelter and there was hell to pay."

"Nearly set the Post Office on fire, too," contributed Crosby.

"Polycarp says all buildings burn well, but Government buildings burn better," said the priest.

Sloan rose dismissively. "I don't think Bonfire Night at the Agricultural Institute will concern us, sir."

Wherein he was wrong.

CHAPTER SIX

It was still damp in the grounds, and for that Sloan was grateful. It meant that the footprints Crosby had found not far from the cellar door were perfectly preserved.

"Two sets, Inspector." He straightened his back. They were in the shelter of one of the large rhododendron bushes. "One of them stood for a while in the same place. The earth's quite soft here. ..." He slipped out a measure. "Men's. ..."

"Perhaps."

"It was a man's shoe, sir ..."

"But was there a man inside it? Don't forget that this lot wear men's shoes—every one of them."

Crosby measured the depth. "If it was a woman, it was a heavy one."

"Get a cast and we'll know for certain." He looked round. "It would be a good enough spot to watch the back of the place from." From where he was standing he could see the kitchen door, the cellar steps, a splendid collection of dustbins and a small glass door which presumably led to the garden room. A broad path led round towards the front entrance of the house, and along this now was walking the Caller, Sister Gertrude.

"Inspector, Mother says will you come please? She's had a letter."

"It was handed to Sister Polycarp a few minutes ago," said the Reverend Mother, "by one of the village children from a gentleman who is staying at The Bull. He says in his letter that he proposes to call at the Convent at four-thirty this afternoon in the hopes of being able to see Sister Anne."

"Does he?" said Sloan with interest. "Who is he?"

The Mother Prioress handed over the letter. "It's signed 'Harold Cartwright.' A relation, presumably."

"Do you know him? Has he been here before?"

She shook her head. "No. I do not recollect Sister Anne having any visitors. Do you, Sister?"

Sister Lucy looked up. "Never, Mother."

"Would she have seen this man in the ordinary way?"

"Not if she did not wish it, Inspector. Nor if I did not wish it. Sometimes visitors are no great help—especially to young postulants and novices, and are therefore not allowed."

"He says here he hopes no objection will be raised to his visit, which is of considerable importance," said Sloan, quoting the letter.

"To him," said the Reverend Mother. "Visitors are rarely important to us. Nevertheless, I think in this instance that we had better ask Sister Polycarp to show him to the Parlor when he comes."

He arrived promptly at four-thirty, a man aged about fifty- five in a dark gray suit. He was heavily built and going gray. He wasted no time in getting to the point.

"I am Harold Cartwright, the cousin of Sister Anne, and I would very much like to see her for a few moments. ..."

"I am afraid," said the Reverend Mother, "that that will not be possible. ..."

"I know," said the man quickly, "that she probably does not wish to see me or any of her family, but it is on a matter of some importance. That is why I have traveled down here in person rather than written to her. ..."

"*When* did you travel down here?" asked Sloan.

Cartwright turned. "Last night. I stayed at The Bull."

"What time did you arrive?"

"Is that any concern of—"

"I am a police officer investigating a sudden death."

"I see." Again the man wasted no time in coming to the point. "I got to The Bull about seven-thirty, had a meal and a drink in the bar and went to bed."

"Straight to bed?"

"No. If you're interested I went for a quick walk round the village to get a breath of air before going to my room."

"I see, sir, thank you."

"Mr. Cartwright," the Mother Prioress inclined her coif slightly, "how long is it since you last saw Sister Anne?"

"Almost twenty years. I went to another Convent to see her. Hersely, it was."

"That would be so. We have a House there."

"I went to ask if there was anything she wanted, anything we could do for her." His mouth twisted. "She said she had everything and I came away again."

"Mr. Cartwright, you must be prepared for a shock."

He laughed shortly. "I know she'll be a changed woman. No one's the same after twenty years. I'm not the same man myself if it comes to that."

The Mother Prioress lowered her head. "I have no doubt that great changes have been wrought by the passage of time in you both but that is not the point. I am sorry to have to tell you that the sudden death into which Inspector Sloan is enquiring is that of your cousin, Sister Anne."

Harold Cartwright sat very still. "You mean Josephine's dead?"

"Yes, Mr. Cartwright."

"When?"

"She died last night."

"Why the police?"

"She was found dead at the foot of a flight of steps."

"An accident, surely?"

"We hope so."

"It couldn't be anything else here. I mean, not in a Convent."

"I would like to think not," agreed the Mother Prioress, "but that matter is not yet resolved."

Cartwright turned to Sloan again. "Why might it not be an accident? Would anyone want to harm my cousin?"

"I don't know, sir. I was hoping that you might be able to tell us."

"Me? I haven't had sight nor sound of her for twenty years."

"You're not her only relation?"

"No. Her father—my uncle—died years ago, but her mother's still alive. …"

"Mrs. Alfred Cartwright, 17 Strelitz Square?"

"That's right. How did you know?"

"The Convent records," said Sloan briefly.

"They didn't get on."

"I inferred that."

"My aunt is a very strong-minded woman. She greatly resented my cousin taking her vows. I don't think she has ever forgiven her."

"I am sure *she* has been forgiven," interposed the Reverend Mother.

"I beg your pardon?"

"By Sister Anne."

"Oh, I see what you mean. Yes, of course." It didn't seem as if Harold Cartwright had thought of this at all. He waved a hand vaguely. "Before she died, you mean. ..."

"Many years ago," said the Mother Prioress firmly. "It would not be possible to live the life of a true religious and harbor that sort of unforgiveness."

"No, no, I can see that."

Sloan coughed. "Now, sir, perhaps you'll tell us what it was that was so important that you had to see her about after all these years."

But that was something Harold Cartwright obviously did not want to do. "What? Oh, yes, of course. What I'd come to see her about?"

"Yes."

"Well, it's not really relevant now she's dead. Just a family matter, that's all. Nothing that would concern anyone now, you understand." He gave a quick smile. "Death cancels all that sort of thing, doesn't it?"

"No," said the Mother Prioress directly. "Not in my experience."

"No? Perhaps not, but it does alter them, and it has altered all I had come to see her about."

Sloan let it ride. This was only the beginning. "Will you be leaving Cullingoak tonight?" he asked him.

"No. Not now—I think I'd better stay on, don't you?" He frowned. "Though there's my aunt. Perhaps I ought to go back to tell her. ..."

"I'll do that," said Sloan suddenly.

Harold Cartwright said, "Thank you." He looked back to the Mother Superior and said diffidently. "There'll be a funeral, I take it—would I be allowed to come to that?"

She nodded briskly. "Of course, Mr. Cartwright. But first there is, I understand, to be a post-mortem. ..."

Cartwright looked quickly at the inspector.

"To establish the exact cause of death," said Sloan.

It was dark when Sloan came out to Cullingoak for the second time that day. There were bonfires and fireworks all about as the police car slipped through the streets of Berebury and out into the open country towards Cullingoak.

"Get a move on, man," he muttered irritably, as Crosby slowed down for a crossroads. He sat beside the constable, his shoulders hunched up, hands sunk deep into his pockets, thinking hard.

As they swept into Cullingoak High Street he heard the clang of a fire engine's bell. He saw the engine careening along ahead of them, firemen pulling on their boots as they clung to the machine. It did a giant swerve and headed unerringly between the gates of the Agricultural Institute. Crosby followed suit and bumped up the drive after the fire engine.

The fire was over on their right, away from the Institute's buildings. It was well alight, with flames leaping high into the air. Standing round it like a votive circle were the students. Their faces stood out in a white ring in the darkness, the dancing flames reflected in them.

Sloan burst from the car and ran over to the fire brigade.

"I want that fire out," he shouted. "Quickly."

"Blimey," said a Leading Fireman. "It's only a bonfire."

"I know it is," snapped Sloan, "but I want it out before the guy is burnt. This is a police matter, so look sharp. I want that guy in one piece whatever happens."

"You'll be lucky," said the man over his shoulder, and was gone.

Round the other side of the fire boys were still feeding the flames, and Sloan shouted at them too.

The fire brigade were running their hoses towards the fire, lacing them in and out of the spectators. The boys divided their attention between them and the fire. The latter was of magnificent proportions now, the flames licking their way to the figure lashed to the top.

There was a sigh from the crowd as the first flame lapped round the feet of the guy.

"Hurry," urged Sloan.

He squinted up through the smoke and blackness. Impossible to tell if the material was alight or not. A tongue of flame ran up behind it towards the head. Sloan very nearly plunged into the flames himself to rescue it.

Suddenly some boys on his left moved quickly to one side and he saw the hose leap into life.

The noise of the bonfire gave way to the noise of water hissing upon flame, and the delectable smell of bonfire was succeeded by an acrid mixture of smoke and steam. The flames fell back.

"Don't hit the guy if you can help it," said Sloan to the man struggling with the hose.

"You don't half want a lot, guv'nor," retorted the man, continuing to play the hose where he wished. "If it falls down in the middle of this you've had it. Besides, a drop of water won't do it no harm, will it? I reckon she was pretty warm where she was."

Minutes later the Leading Fireman came up to him with the guy lying in his arms.

"Daftest rescue job I've ever done, but here you are."

Sloan found himself nursing the damp, faintly charred effigy of a nun. There was a pair of spectacles tied ridiculously across the mock face.

A man came up to him. "Inspector? I'm Marwin Ranby, the Principal of the Institute. I'm very sorry about all this. I feel I'm in some way to blame. You see, last year …"

"I know all about last year," said Sloan grimly.

He had just seen a sight which made him feel very uneasy indeed: Harold Cartwright.

Marwin Ranby led the way into his study. He was hovering round the forty mark, Sloan decided, with a head of fair hair that made him seem younger than he probably was. The study was a pleasant room, with a fire burning at one end, a sofa and chairs round it. At the other end was a desk and bookshelves loaded with heavy agricultural tomes. Over the fireplace hung a Rowland Ward, and in one corner was a tray set with decanter and glasses.

Ranby waved Sloan to a chair and made for these.

"What will you have, Inspector? No? You don't mind if I do, do you?" He groaned. "I don't know what's going to happen when Celia hears about this. Or the Mother Superior."

Sloan laid his burden down on the sofa as tenderly as if she had been human. It wouldn't do the chintz much good, but Ranby wasn't in a position to complain.

"I blame myself," went on the Principal. "I gated them, you know, because of last year. I hoped that way we could minimize any damage done. You'd have thought that bus shelter was an Ancient Monument the way the bus company carried on. And look what happens." He stared at the guy and shuddered. "I'm to be married at the end of the month in the Convent Chapel by special permission of goodness knows who, and they go and burn a nun on Guy Fawkes' Night. What will Celia—Miss Faine, you know—say? And what will the Mother Prioress think?"

He started to pace up and down. Sloan examined the guy closely. The habit was genuine and it was the same as that worn by the nuns next door. The face had been made out of an old stocking, stuffed, with a couple of black buttons sewn on for eyes and the glasses kept on over these with a piece of string tying the ends together at the back. The rest of the habit was spread over a tightly stuffed large sack. No attempt had been made to make feet, and the figure—squat and dumpy—had a distinct resemblance to that of Queen Victoria towards the end of her Sixty Glorious Years.

"I suppose I should have expected something like this," said Ranby after a minute or two. "They are none of them old. Besides, they took the news of the gating too well."

"When did you tell them, sir?"

"After supper on Sunday evening." He laughed shortly. "Gave them a day or so to hatch something up. She smells a bit, doesn't she?"

"The flames caught a little."

"Inspector …"

"Sir?"

"Don't think me inquisitive but how did you come to hear about this? You're from Berebury, aren't you?"

"That's right, sir. Someone telephoned us."

"The devil they did! Who on earth would do that? And why?"

"The caller didn't leave his name, sir. Just said he thought we'd be interested."

"But why? It's not a crime, is it, to burn a guy? Or is it sedition? Or an anti-Popish Plot or something obscure like that?"

"No, sir, not that I know of."

"Well, Inspector, while I don't blame you for rescuing it, I'm not sure that it might not have been better from my point of view if it had been burnt to cinders. Then there would have been no chance of either the Big House or the Dower House seeing." He finished his drink. "But they'd have heard in the end, I suppose."

"Do you know which of your students would have been responsible for this—the idea, getting the habit and so forth?"

"No." The Principal frowned. "We've got about a hundred and fifty men here with about a dozen natural leaders among them. They're here for three years, but the freshmen have only been in residence a month, so I would say a second- or third-year man for sure. That's a point. The habit … Don't say they took that from the Convent!" He ran his hands through his hair. "I'd never live that down. But they couldn't, Inspector. How would they get in or out?"

"I don't know if the habit came from there or not, sir, but I will find out presently."

"And I'll find out the man responsible for the guy and take him round to the Convent in the morning to apologize. I think I'd better tell Miss Faine myself. She's a very devout girl, you know."

"She didn't come round this evening?"

"No, thank God. No, she's gone to London for the day to have a fitting for her dress."

Sloan straightened up. "Thank you, sir, you've been most helpful. There's just one thing. This ringleader. I want to talk to him myself—before anyone on the staff, I mean. That's important."

"I'm a bit bewildered, Inspector, but if that's how you want it, I'll track him down and send him to you."

"If you would. My constable's already seeing how far he can get tonight."

"Is he?" Marwin Ranby looked momentarily annoyed, and then smiled again. "Perhaps he'll be successful, though I fear we both represent authority. But, Inspector, why this interest in a guy? It's not usual for the police to—"

"Hadn't you heard, sir? One of the Sisters at the Convent died last night from injuries that we can't immediately account for."

"No!" He looked down at the travesty on the sofa. "We are in trouble then. That makes this very much worse, doesn't it?"

"More interesting, too, sir, wouldn't you say? Now, if you would just hold the door open I'll put her in the car."

The fire brigade had gone now and a few boys were trying to coax the damp fire back into life. Crosby loomed up out of the near darkness and helped Sloan lay the guy on the back seat of the police car.

"Watch her carefully, Crosby."

"Inspector Bring-'em-back-alive," murmured Crosby, but fortunately Sloan was out of earshot. He was stumbling among the trees looking for Harold Cartwright. He found him at the far corner of the reviving fire and drew him to one side.

"There's just one question I want to ask you, sir. Did you or did you not telephone us about this guy?"

"Me, Inspector? No. No, I heard about it in The Bull and came along to see what was going on. I would have rung you as soon as I saw the guy, of course, if I hadn't heard the fire siren."

"Of course."

Cartwright gave him a tight smile. "I'm glad to see the Lady's Not for Burning. Funny thing for them to do, wasn't it?"

"Very." Sloan stumped back to the car and climbed in beside Crosby. He sniffed. "Something's burning—the guy. …"

"No, sir, it's me." Crosby flushed in the darkness. "A jumping cracker. One of the little perishers tied it to my coat."

"Get him?"

"No."

"Let's hope it's not an augury, that's all."

CHAPTER SEVEN

Back in Berebury Sloan dissected the guy with the same care that Dr. Dabbe had gone about his postmortem. He was joined by Superintendent Leeyes.

"Who is this man Cartwright?" he demanded.

"He says he's her cousin, sir."

"And he just appears out of the blue asking to see her the afternoon after she's killed when he hasn't seen her for twenty years?"

"Yes, sir."

"What does he want to do that for?"

"I don't know yet, sir."

"Find out about him for a start. If he hadn't come to the Convent this afternoon was there anything to connect him with this woman?"

"Only his name and address in the hotel register. It needn't have been the right one but it was."

"So he has a reason—a good reason—for coming, Sloan, hasn't he? Otherwise he would have cleared off as soon as he could." Leeyes grunted. "Perhaps it was to make sure she was dead."

"Or that he'd clobbered the right one."

"If he'd waited to hear in the ordinary way about that death he might have waited quite a while, of course. There's no obligation on their part to tell anyone, I suppose." He shrugged his shoulders. "They call it a Living Death so perhaps there's not a lot of difference."

"We've got a lead, anyway, which is something. I'll go to see the mother in the morning and also find out a bit more about this man. We've checked on The Bull already. He arrived at about seven-thirty, spent an hour over his meal, had a couple of drinks in the bar and then went out for a stroll."

The superintendent's head went up. "When did you say she was last seen alive?"

"About a quarter to nine—at the end of Vespers."

"When did he get back?"

"The landlord didn't notice. Says he was busy with the usual crowd."

"What's he like?"

"Not a fool."

The superintendent wasn't a fool either. "What was he doing at this bonfire?"

Sloan shook his head. "I don't know, sir."

"And who rang here and told us about it?"

"A man's voice, it was, but that's all that switchboard can tell us."

Leeyes indicated the guy. "Someone wanted us to see this before it was burnt to a cinder. Why?"

"I don't know, sir. Not yet. There's one thing—the footprints we found weren't Cartwright's."

"Those glasses—are they the missing ones?"

"I don't know that either, sir, yet." Sloan undid them very carefully. "We'll try them for fingerprints, but I doubt if we'll get anything worth while." He undid the habit and coif and slipped them off, leaving a large stuffed farm sack lying on the bench. The habit, deeply scorched in places, was old and darned. He felt its thinness between his fingers.

Superintendent Leeyes grunted. "I don't get it, Sloan. This woman, Sister Anne, she wasn't naked or anything?"

"Oh, no, sir," said Sloan, deeply shocked. "It's not that sort of place at all."

"Perhaps she was killed in her Number Ones," said Leeyes. "Or perhaps this tomfoolery has got nothing whatsoever to do with it and you're wasting your time, Sloan. In that case," he fingered the charred habit, "it would seem that the wrong one's wearing the sackcloth and ashes—eh?"

"Yes, sir," said Sloan dutifully.

Sloan had been married for fifteen years.

Long enough to view his wife's nightly ritual with face cream with patient indifference.

Long enough for her to be surprised as he slipped into bed beside her when he pulled the white sheet right round and across the top of her forehead.

"Denis, what on earth are you doing?"

He tucked the blanket as far under her chin as it would go and considered her.

"That's all you can see of a nun."

"I should think so, too. What more do you want?"

"Funny what a good idea of a woman you can get from this bit."

She shook her head. "Don't you believe it, dear. Men always think that. It's not true."

"No gray now."

"Beast," retorted his wife equably. "On the other hand, you can't see my ankles." Margaret Sloan had very good ankles and very little gray hair.

He relaxed his hold on the sheet and lay on his back. "Margaret …"

"Well?"

"What would make a woman go into a convent?"

"Don't they call it having a vocation or something? Like nursing or teaching."

"They can't all have felt a call, can they? There's over fifty of them there."

"I don't know," she said doubtfully. "Perhaps they were religious-minded anyway and then something happened to drive them there."

"Like what—as Crosby would say?"

"Being lonely, would you think, or jilted perhaps, or the man in their life loving another. That sort of thing." She tugged at the pillow. "Or not having any man there in the first place, of course."

Sloan yawned. "Escape, too, would you say? Not facing up to things. Running away from life."

"There's always that, I suppose."

"Not my idea of a life. The superintendent called it a living death." He pulled the eiderdown up. "Can't see you going in one either, dear."

"Oh, I don't know," said his wife.

"What do you mean?"

"Suppose something had happened to you after we got engaged. What should I have done then, do you think? A living death wouldn't have mattered very much then, would it?"

He turned to face her, oddly disconcerted. "I … I hadn't thought of that."

She snuggled down in the bed. "Mind you," she said sleepily, "I don't think I would have made a very good nun."

Marwin Ranby's study at the Agricultural Institute looked almost as comfortable in daylight as it had done in the cozy, shaded light of last evening. There was a young woman with him. She had pale auburn hair and the delicate, almost translucent skin that often goes with it. The clothes she was wearing were deceptively, ridiculously simple, and Sloan was not at all surprised to find himself being introduced to Miss Celia Faine, the last of her line and Marwin Ranby's fiancée.

"I have been telling Miss Faine something of last night's excitement," said the Principal.

"But, I suspect, not everything," said Celia Faine with a smile. She had a pleasant, unaffected voice. "Marwin's being very discreet, Inspector."

"I'm glad to hear it, miss," responded Sloan.

"Or should I say 'mysterious'? It's because he thinks I should mind. But I know his boys get up to all sorts of things. They wouldn't be boys if they didn't, would they? I don't think the Sisters would mind either if they did hear about it—they're perfectly sweet, you know, and so—sort of balanced, if you know what I mean. You feel they are finished with the petty, trivial things that don't matter. It isn't as if it was a demonstration against them or anything. Nobody minded them coming to Cullingoak, and we had to do something with the house. In fact, I think people are glad they're there in a way."

"Celia thinks their sanctity balances out the devilment in my young men," said Ranby lightly, matching her tone, "but I'm not so sure myself. Until last night I wouldn't have thought they were even aware of them. We hear their bell on a clear day—that usually provokes a crack or two about getting the cows in—but nothing more."

"What about last night?" asked Sloan.

"No news, Inspector. None of my staff knew anything about the guy."

"You have other means of finding out?"

"Naturally. I can if necessary interview the whole lot, but that takes time. I was hoping to appeal to them at supper tonight—it's the first meal that they will all be at together. I have already checked that no one had a late pass on Wednesday night."

"Is that infallible? My experience is that it isn't as a rule."

"Rumor has it the Biology Laboratory window can be persuaded to open if pressure is judiciously applied in the right place."

"I'll get my constable to fingerprint it straight away."

"You really want this chap, don't you?"

"Yes," said Sloan shortly. "We do."

Strelitz Square was still a square in the sense that its Georgian creator had intended, and there was still a garden in the middle. The houses were tall, dignified and—most significant of all—still lived in. Number Seventeen was on the north side, facing the thin November sun. Sloan and Crosby rang the bell at exactly ten-thirty the next morning. An elderly aproned maid answered the door.

He didn't mention the Convent this time. "Detective- Inspector Sloan," he said, "would be obliged if Mrs. Cartwright would spare him a moment or two."

The woman looked them over appraisingly and then invited them in. She would enquire if Mrs. Cartwright was at home.

"Funny way of carrying on," said Crosby.

"You're in Society now, constable, and don't you forget it. Plenty of money here." Sloan looked quickly round the room into which they had been shown. "Pictures, china, furniture—the lot."

Crosby fingered a finely carved chair. "Is this fashion, sir?"

"It was," said Sloan, "about two hundred years ago. It's antique, like everything else in the room." He pointed to a set of Dresden shepherdesses. "They'll be worth more than your pension. Don't suppose they picked up that walnut bureau for five bob either or those plates …"

"Good morning, Inspector." An elderly figure appeared in the doorway. "Admiring my Meissen? Charming, isn't it?"

"Good morning, madam," said Sloan, not committing himself about the Meissen, whatever that was.

Mrs. Cartwright was old, ramrod-backed and thin. She rested a claw-like hand on the back of the chair just long enough for Sloan to see the battery of rings on it and then she sat down. She was dressed—and dressed very well indeed—in gray with touches of scarlet. Sloan searched her face for a likeness to Sister Anne but found only heavy makeup and the tiny suture marks of an old facelift. Her hair was a deep mahogany color and the total effect quite startling.

"You have something to say, Inspector."

"Yes, madam." Sloan jerked his mind back. She must be over eighty, and he thought he had bad news for her. "I understand you had a telephone call yesterday afternoon from the Convent of St. Anselm."

Not a muscle on her face moved.

"And that you refused to take that call."

"That is so." Her voice was harsher than he expected.

"Why, madam?"

"Is it anything to do with you?"

"I'm afraid it is."

"Really, Inspector, I can see no reason why ..."

"You had a daughter there."

Mrs. Cartwright rose and walked towards a bell by the fireplace. "I have no daughter."

"One moment, madam. You are quite right ..."

She stopped and looked at him.

"You have no daughter. But you had one."

She stood rigidly in front of the fireplace and said again in a well-controlled voice, "I have no daughter." She put her finger towards the bell.

"Mrs. Cartwright!"

"Well?" Her finger was poised.

"You had a daughter called Josephine Mary."

A spasm of emotion passed across her face. "Inspector, I lost my daughter thirty years ago."

"Lost her?"

"Lost her. She left me, she left everything." Mrs. Cartwright waved a painted fingernail round the room. "Abandoned. Moreover, Inspector, her name has not been mentioned in this house from that day to this. I see no reason to discontinue the habit. Now, if you will either state your business or leave."

"When did you last see her, madam?"

"The day she left home."

"Thirty years ago?"

"Thirty-one. She was eighteen and a half."

So Sister Anne had been forty-nine. She hadn't looked as old as that.

"And you, madam, hadn't seen her yourself since then?" Sloan hoped he was keeping the wonder out of his voice.

"Not once. I told her that she needn't expect me to visit her. And I never did."

"Had—have you any other children?"

"She was the only one, Inspector, and she left me. She was a convert, of course. Nothing would persuade her. Nothing." The old eyes danced. "She wanted to eschew the World, the Flesh and the Devil, Inspector, and she did. At eighteen and a half, without knowing anything about any of the three of them. I hope she's enjoyed it, that's all. Being walled up with a lot of other women praying all day long instead of getting married and having children. What's she done, Inspector? Run away after all these years?"

"No, madam."

"Because if she has, you needn't come looking for her here." There was a gleam of satisfaction in her voice. "She wouldn't come back here, Inspector. I can tell you that. Not if it was the last place on earth."

"No, madam, it's not that at all. ..."

"Don't say she's done something wrong! That I would find hard to believe. I shouldn't imagine you arrest many nuns, Inspector, but if she was one of them I must say I would derive a certain amount of amusement from the fact. She was so very pious."

"I've come to tell you that she's dead."

The old mouth tightened. "She died as far as I'm concerned the day she left home."

"And that she was probably murdered."

"Poor Josephine," she said grimly. "She didn't escape the wicked world after all then, did she, Inspector?"

They were back in Berebury by lunchtime.

"Get anywhere?" asked Superintendent Leeyes.

"I don't know," said Sloan. "Can't say I blame her for leaving home. I'd have gone myself. Mother hasn't seen her for thirty years—or so she says anyway."

"Check on that."

"Lots and lots of money there."

The superintendent's head came up. "Is there now? Check on that, too, Sloan. Money is a factor in the crime equation."

"Yes, sir." Last winter the superintendent had attended a course on "Mathematics for the Average Adult." It had left its mark.

"Who inherits?"

"I'll find out."

Leeyes looked sharply across at him. "It could be the Convent, I suppose?"

"Not now she's dead, would you think?"

"Perhaps not. It would be interesting to know if she would have inherited had she lived. This mother—is she old?"

"Very. And she wouldn't have made her the sole heir—not from the way she was talking."

"Cut off with the proverbial shilling, eh?"

"Yes, sir."

Leeyes grunted. "She mightn't have had any say. She a widow?"

"Yes."

"Where does cousin Harold come in then?"

"I don't know yet."

"Find out then, man. It could be important."

"Yes, sir."

"And find out who gets it if the Convent doesn't. That could be important, too." He drummed his fingers on the desk. "I don't suppose you'll get out of anyone at the Convent what sort of dowry Sister Anne brought with her."

"Dowry?"

"Gifts in money or kind brought to a marriage contract, Sloan. They have the same custom when a girl goes into a Convent. In India it's a couple of cows or some sheep. My father-in-law gave me some dud shares."

Sloan flushed. There had been a pair of brass candlesticks that his wife had brought from her home, ugly as sin, that had dominated the mantel-piece of their best room all their married life. "I know what you mean, sir. I'll try to find out."

"Of course," said Leeyes, off now on a different tack, "this lot may have taken vows of perpetual poverty or something idiotic like that."

"I hope not," said Sloan piously. "Upset all the usual motives too much, that would."

"What's that? Yes, it would. We must hope that they haven't done anything so foolish."

Sloan went back to his own room.

Crosby came in. "Dr. Dabbe wants to talk to you, sir, and there's a message from the Convent."

Sloan lifted his head. "Well?"

"Please may they have their keys back?"

CHAPTER EIGHT

An unused knife, fork, spoon and table napkin marked the place at the refectory table where Sister Anne had sat for most of her religious life. Sister Michael and Sister Damien sat on either side of the gap—the one professed immediately before Sister Anne, and the other immediately after. It was the midday meal and the Reader was pursuing her way through the Martyrology.

The vicissitudes of the early faithful seemed to be as nothing compared with the trials of working through today's pudding. A reasonable stew had been eaten with the relish of those who have been up since very early morning, but today's pudding was obviously different.

Custom decreed that it should be eaten (many a martyr had died of starvation—or poison); their creed forbade criticism. So fifty-odd nuns struggled with a doughy indefinable mixture lacking the main ingredients of a sweet course.

Sister Cellarer was at the Parlor door immediately the meal was finished.

"Mother, I hope I am lacking in neither ingenuity nor humility but I find it exceedingly difficult to cook without the basic essentials."

"Not ingenuity, my child. No one could say that."

Sister Cellarer flushed. "It's quite impossible to …"

"Nothing is impossible, Sister. It may be difficult but impossible is a word no true religious should use lightly."

"No, Mother." Sister Cellarer lowered her eyes. "I'm sorry …"

"As to humility, I'm not sure." The Mother Prioress contemplated the hot and ruffled cook. "Did you feel the Community would blame you for the shortcomings of our dinner? If so, Sister, I suggest you examine your motives in complaining. I think if you look at them closely you will find an element of pride. Pride in personal skill is a dangerous matter in a Convent. All work and skill here should be offered to our Lord from whom our strength to do it comes. The sin of pride is not one I should have to look for in you."

A diminished Sister Cellarer was on her knees. "I ask forgiveness, Mother. I should have thought."

The Mother Prioress waved a hand. "May God bless you, Sister. As it happens I have sent a message about the keys, but it may well be that we will not have them yet. I can see that the police would need to know if they had any significance."

"They didn't have anything to do with Sister Anne at all," said Sister Cellarer. "Sister Lucy lent them to her just for the evening."

"I have told them that," said the Reverend Mother patiently, "but until they know how it was that Sister Anne died I think they are justified in retaining them."

Sister Cellarer rose. "Of course," she said soberly. "That is what matters. Poor Sister Anne. It doesn't seem possible that only the day before yesterday none of this had happened at all."

"The day before yesterday seems a very long time ago now." The Mother Prioress gathered her habit up preparatory to going somewhere at her usual speed. "Will you ask the Sacrist to come to see me in the Chapel, and the Chantress, too, if she's about?"

Sloan got Dr. Dabbe on the telephone.

"Sister Anne died from a depressed fracture of the skull," said the doctor, "caused by the application of the traditional blunt instrument. She had a postmortem fracture of her right femur almost certainly caused by the fall down the cellar steps, and also sundry hematoma …"

"Heema what?"

"Bruises. Also mostly caused after death. You don't bleed much then, of course."

"No."

"I would say she was hit from behind and slightly above—perhaps by someone taller."

"Man or woman?" asked Sloan eagerly, and got the usual medical prevarication.

"Difficult to say, Inspector. She wasn't hit so hard that only a man could have done it—on the other hand there were unusual features. The coif, for instance, and the complete absence of hair. It was a heavy blow, but in a good position with a wide swing it wouldn't have been out of the question for a woman—especially a tall one."

"Weapon?"

"You want to look for something round and smooth and heavy."

Sloan flipped over a page of his notebook. "Time of death?"

"Between six and seven night before last."

"*When?*"

"I can't tell you to the minute, you know. Let's put it this way—she had been dead approximately sixteen to seventeen hours when I saw her just after eleven o'clock yesterday morning."

"But they have supper at quarter past six and—"

"She'd had supper," said the pathologist laconically. "She died on a full stomach, if that's any consolation to anybody. The meal was quite undigested. Shouldn't have fancied it myself. Too many peas."

Sloan turned back to his notebook. "But she was at some service or other—I've got it here—Vespers—at half past eight."

"Not if she had steak and kidney pudding and peas at six- fifteen," said the pathologist. "The process of digestion had barely started. I'll put it all in writing for you."

"Thank you. This alters some of my ideas."

"Postmortems usually do."

Sloan set down the telephone receiver very thoughtfully indeed.

Sister Polycarp satisfied herself with a quicker scrutiny this time. "It's yourself, Inspector. And the constable. Come in. You'll be wanting the Parlor, I suppose?" She shut the grille and appeared in person through one of the doors. "This way. Mother Prioress is in the Chapel but Sister Lucy will see you."

They followed her through to the Parlor.

"I don't suppose you show many men through these doors," ventured Sloan tentatively.

"The plumber," said Polycarp tartly. "Can't do without him, and the doctor. He comes to see old Mother Thérèse."

"What about the Agricultural Institute? Do you have any visitors from there?"

She shook her head. "That we do not. Young limbs of Satan, that's what students are."

"What about Mr. Ranby?"

"Oh, he came the other day to see about the wedding. I took him through to the Parlor to talk to Reverend Mother and the Sacrist. We haven't had a wedding here before, you see. I think Mr. Ranby comes to the Chapel, too, but of course I hadn't seen him before."

"Why 'of course'?"

She stared at him. "The grille. Across the Chapel. Haven't you been in there?"

"Yes, I saw the grille."

"Well, the Community sits in front and then there's this screen and then the public."

"So you can't see them?"

"Naturally not."

"And they can't see you?"

"Of course not. That wouldn't be proper, would it?"

"Therefore you have no idea at all who comes in at the back?"

"Except that they are local people who always come—no. I open the side door before the service and lock it up afterwards."

"Every time?"

She looked him straight in the eye. "Every time, Inspector. And I do a round of doors and windows last thing at night."

"When would that be?"

"Eight o'clock."

Sloan reckoned he had been in short trousers when eight o'clock had been "last thing at night."

"And Hobbett?"

"He comes and goes according to his work and the weather. He has his own key to the boiler room."

Polycarp shut the Parlor door behind them.

Crosby tapped the bare, polished floor with his foot and pointed to the plain walls. "Bit of a change from Strelitz Square for that Sister Anne."

"I expect that's why she came."

Sister Lucy came into the Parlor with Sister Gertrude. They bowed slightly, then sat down, hands clasped together in front, and looked at him expectantly.

Sloan undid a brown-paper parcel he had brought with him.

"This habit. Can you tell me anything about it?"

Sister Lucy leaned forward, and Sloan got a good look at her face for the first time. The bone structure was perfect. He didn't know about Sister Anne, but Sister Lucy would have cut quite a figure in a drawing room. He tried to imagine hair where there was only a white coif now. With Sister Gertrude it was easier. Hers was the round jolly face of a "good sort," the games mistress at a girls' school, the unmarried daughter ...

"Yes, Inspector, I think I can." Sister Lucy's voice was quiet and unaccented. "This is the spare habit that we keep in the flower room. Should any Sister get wet while out in the grounds she can slip this on instead while she asks permission to dry her own habit in the laundry. It is kept behind the door on a hook." She turned it round expertly. "You see, here is the hook. It is very old and worn now, but none the less blessed for that."

"Thank you, Sister. Now take a look at these."

"Sister Anne's glasses!" Sister Lucy and Sister Gertrude crossed themselves in unison.

"You both confirm that?"

The two nuns nodded. Sister Lucy said, "She wore particularly thick glasses, Inspector. I think she is the only member of the Community with them as thick as that." Her hand disappeared inside her habit and emerged again. "Most of us wear glasses like these. For reading and sewing, you know, but Sister Anne had poor eyesight. She couldn't see anything at all without her glasses."

"Thank you, Sisters. You have been very helpful."

They acknowledged this with another slight bow. ("Like talking to a couple of Chinese mandarins," said Sloan later.)

"Now I would like to tell the Mother Prioress where they were found."

"She is in the Chapel," volunteered Sister Lucy, "arranging the Requiem Mass for Sister Anne. And the Great Office of the Dead. When a Sister dies violently there are certain changes in the responses and so forth."

Sloan permitted himself a bleak smile. "That can't happen often."

"On the contrary, Inspector. We sang just the same service at Midsummer."

"You did? Who for?"

"Sister St. John of the Cross."

"Why?"

"She was hacked to death with a machete."

"What! Where?"

"Unggadinna."

Sloan breathed again. "That's different."

A faint chill came into the atmosphere. "Not so very different, Inspector, for us."

"There was Mother St. Theobald, too, just after Easter," put in Sister Gertrude diffidently. "I was a novice when she was professed so I remember her well. She died in prison, you know, in Communist hands."

"We assumed," said Sister Lucy astringently, "that she died violently, though we have had no exact details yet."

"I'm sorry," said Sloan awkwardly.

"And, of course," persisted Sister Lucy, "there are members of our Order who *were* in China. We have no means of knowing whether or not they are accomplished among the elect." They rose. "We will see if Mother has finished in the Chapel. ..."

Crosby stirred in his hard chair. "Funny thing, sir. They don't ask any questions. Most people would have wanted to know where you got those glasses and that gown thing, wouldn't they?"

"Unless they knew."

"I hadn't thought of that."

The Mother Prioress came back with Sister Lucy. "You have news for us, Inspector?"

"I don't know if it is news or not, marm, but we think Sister Anne was murdered."

He was conscious of Sister Lucy's sharp indrawn breath, but the Reverend Mother only nodded.

"No, Inspector, that is not news. Father MacAuley had already intimated to me that Sister Anne died an unnatural death. He has also told me about last night's bonfire."

"Sister Lucy has just identified the habit and Sister Anne's glasses."

"How very curious that both should be found on a guy at the Agricultural Institute. Do you connect them with Sister Anne's death?"

"I can't say, marm, at this stage. The glasses were hers, she couldn't see without them; she was killed on Wednesday evening, and on Thursday evening they were found on this guy."

"If," said the Mother Prioress slowly, "the whole episode of the guy had been an anti-papist demonstration we, as a Community, would have been aware of feelings against us. After all, they are quite common. Sisters in our other Houses have them to contend with—but not without knowing the feelings existed. Hate is so very communicable. Mr. Ranby would have known, too, I think."

"Granted, marm. But somebody took both the old habit and the glasses."

She inclined her head. "It would seem that the world has been to us or that one of us has been into the world."

Sloan had reached this conclusion himself the evening before and turned to another matter.

"Going back to Sister Anne, herself, marm, can you tell me anything about her? As a person, I mean."

The Mother Prioress smiled faintly. "We try so very hard not to be persons here, you know. To conquer the self and to submerge the personality are part of our daily battle with ourselves in the quest for true humility. I would say that Sister Anne, God rest her soul, succeeded as well as any of us."

"Er—yes, I see." It was patent that he didn't. "Now about her actual death. Did anyone stand to gain by that?"

"Just Sister Anne."

"Sis …"

"It is part of our conviction, Inspector, that all true Christians stand to gain by death."

He smiled weakly. "Of course. But apart from Sister Anne herself?"

"I cannot conceive that anyone could gain from her death."

"In the worldly sense, perhaps?"

"I take it that you mean financially? That is what people usually mean."

"Yes."

"The disposition of any material wealth would be entirely a matter for the Sister concerned."

"Was Sister Anne wealthy?"

"I have no idea, Inspector."

"She came from a wealthy home."

"That is not always a measure."

"Who would know?"

"Just the Mother Prioress at the time she took her vows."

"And that was?"

"Mother Helena …"

"And she's dead?"

"… of blessed memory," finished the Mother Prioress simultaneously.

That meant the same thing. Sloan was getting frustrated. "Is there no way of finding out?"

Sister Lucy coughed. "Mother, the Bursar's accounts. They might show something at the time. We know the date of profession. It would take a little while, but if a dowry had been received it would show in the figures."

"Thank you," said Sloan, taking the Mother Prioress's concurrence for granted. "That would be a great help. Now, what about a will?"

"That," said the Reverend Mother, "would be at our Mother House. It is no part of our intention not to conform to the Common Law of the land in which our House is situated."

"Quite."

"Sister Lucy shall telephone them for you presently."

"Marm, there's another matter that has been troubling us. You told me that Sister Anne was at Chapel on Wednesday evening and that that was the last time she was seen alive."

"That is so. At Vespers by Sister Michael and Sister Damien."

"Do you remember what you had for supper on Wednesday?"

It was clear that she didn't. She turned to Sister Lucy, who frowned. "It wasn't a fast day, Mother. Was it steak and kidney pudding? I think it was. Yes, I'm sure. With peas and potatoes. And then a bread and butter pudding."

"Thank you. Yes, I remember now. Is it important, Inspector?"

"What time did you have it?"

"At a quarter past six. That is when we always have it."

"And then is when Sister Anne had hers?"

"Yes, naturally."

"She couldn't have had hers later?"

"Not without my knowing."

"What happens immediately after supper?"

"Recreation. From a quarter to seven to eight o'clock. Sisters bring any sewing or similar work to the old drawing room and they are permitted to move about and talk there as they wish."

"I see," said Sloan. Nice for them, that was. "And then?"

"They have various minor duties—preparing the refectory for breakfast, locking up the house, general tidying up at the end of the day and so forth. As they finish these the Sisters go into the Chapel for private meditation until Vespers at eight- thirty."

"Thank you, marm, that is what I wanted to know. And Sister Damien and Sister Michael sat on either side of Sister Anne at Vespers?"

"That is so."

"With the greatest respect, marm, that is not so. Dr. Dabbe, the pathologist, tells me that Sister Anne died immediately after supper. Her meal was quite undigested."

There was a silence in the Parlor, then, "Someone sat between Sister Michael and Sister Damien."

"So you tell us, marm."

"So they told me, Inspector."

"Where was Sister Anne's place in the Chapel?"

"In the back row."

"No one else need have noticed her then?"

"No. No, I suppose not. As I said, the Sisters come in when they are ready and kneel until the service begins."

"I think we should see the Chapel and the two Sisters."

"Certainly. Sister Lucy will take you there now."

The Mother Prioress sat on in the empty Parlor, deep in thought. She almost didn't hear the light tap on the door. She roused herself automatically. "Come in."

It was Sister Cellarer. "Did he bring the keys, Mother?"

She stared at her. "Do you know, Sister, I quite forgot to ask him."

CHAPTER NINE

Father MacAuley was the next visitor to the Parlor. Sister Gertrude brought him along.

"I had quite a job getting in. Polycarp thought I was the Press at first. I'll have to have a password. 'Up the Irish' or some such phrase pleasing to her ear."

"There were two reporters and a cameraman this morning," said the Mother Prioress, "but she sent them away."

"So she told me. She didn't know if the photographer got his picture of her or not before she shut the grille. The flash, she said, reminded her of the dear old days in Ireland. Apparently the last really good flash she saw was the day the I.R.A. blew up the bridge at—"

"I have warned the Community," continued the Mother Prioress, "that they may have to go in the grounds in pairs as a precaution against their being—shall we say, surprised—by reporters. I feel there will be more of them."

"They do hunt in packs as a rule."

"Also there has been what I understand is called a new development in the case."

"There has?"

"The pathologist has said that Sister Anne died immediately after supper which finishes at a quarter to seven. Sister Michael and Sister Damien say she sat between them at Vespers at eight-thirty."

The priest nodded sagely. "The Press would like that."

"I do not, Father. The implications are very disturbing. If Sister Anne was dead at half past eight, who sat in her stall at Vespers?"

The priest sat down heavily. "I don't know. The fact that we do not believe in—er—manifestations will scarcely influence the public—who don't know what they believe in. They, and therefore the Press, dearly love a ghost. Can't you see the headlines?"

The Mother Prioress winced.

In intervals between inspecting the Convent Chapel, Sloan took one telephone call and made another from the old-fashioned instrument in the corridor. Both were London calls, but neither would have conveyed very much to Mrs. Briggs at the Cullingoak Post Office, who monitored all calls as a matter of course.

"With reference to your enquiry," said the London voice, "we have found a very interesting will in Somerset House, made by one Alfred Cartwright, father of Josephine Mary Cartwright. It was made a long time ago, and, in fact, several years before his death. Sounds as if he and his brother Joe were pretty cautious blokes. They'd got everything worked out carefully enough. If Alfred died first his widow was to have the income from his share of the Consolidated Carbon partnership for her lifetime. If he had children they were to get the share when their mother died. If he didn't have any children or if those children predeceased him *or* his brother, Joe, then the share in the Cartwright patent was to go to Joe and then his heirs and successors."

"Keeping it in the family," said Sloan.

"That's the spirit, old chap. Well, they seem to have gone along fairly slowly with the business—all this was just after the old Queen died, remember. Turn of the century and all that. Then suddenly—and without any warning either—Alfred ups and dies. Pneumonia, it was. We looked up the death certificate, too, while we were about it. ..."

"Thank you."

"He doesn't leave very much but not to worry. Not many years afterwards along comes World War One and Cartwright's Consolidated Carbons can't help making money. Lots and lots of it. Of course, our Alfred doesn't get the benefit being dead by now, but the stuff keeps on coming in. Must have been pretty well running out of their ears by 1918."

"What about brother Joe?"

"There's no will registered of his, so presumably he's still alive. He probably made a reciprocal will at the same time as his brother, but of course he could have altered it since. ... By the way, we confirm Mrs. Alfred Cartwright's statement that there was only one child of the marriage. This girl Josephine. Her husband died soon after the baby was born."

"And brother Joe?"

"He had one son by the name of Harold. He must be all of fifty-five now."

"We've met son Harold." A thought struck Sloan. "So Joe Cartwright will be quite an age."

"Practically gaga, I should say," said the voice helpfully.

"What about the firm now?"

"Ah, you want he whom we call our City Editor. I'm only an historian. Fred Jenkins is the chap for the up-to-the-minute stuff. The only police- man who does his beat in striped pants and a bowler. No truncheon either. Says his umbrella's better. I'll give you his number."

"Much obliged," said Sloan. He rang it immediately.

"Cartwright's Consolidated Carbons? Very sound, Inspector. Good family firm. A bit old-fashioned but most good old family firms are these days. Well run, all the same. Not closed minds, if you know what I mean. They're not entirely convinced that one computer will do the work of fifty men, but if you prove it to them they'll buy the computer and see the fifty men don't suffer for it."

"The family still manage it?"

"Lord, yes. Harold Cartwright's the M.D. Knows the business back- wards. Learned it the hard way, I should say. Let me see now, I think there are two sons and a daughter. That's right. The daughter married well. Iron ore, I think it was. The boys went to a good school and an even better university. The elder boy had a year at Harvard to see what our American cousins could teach him about business, and the younger one a year on the Rand."

"You know a lot about them off the cuff."

"One of the largest *private* companies in the country, Inspector, that's why," retorted Jenkins promptly. "They're always getting write-ups in the City pages suggesting they will be going public but they never do. They'd be quite a good buy when the time comes, of course, that's why there's the interest."

"I think," said Sloan slowly, "I can tell you the reason why they've stayed private all these years."

There was no mistaking the interest at the other end of the line. "You can?"

"There was a residual legatee here in Calleshire in a convent." There was a lot of satisfaction in being able to tell London something.

"That's it then. What sort of share?"

"If she survived her uncle I'd say she was stuck in for half."

Jenkins whistled. "Buying her out would upset the applecart. I don't suppose they would have enough liquidity to do it. That's the trouble with that sort of heavy industry. On the other hand, if they go public and leave her in they could be in a mess. They might lose control, you see. Tricky."

"Not quite so tricky now," said Sloan. "She was killed on Wednesday evening. I don't know how these things are managed, but I would like to know if this question of going public comes up again now."

"I'll have a poke round the Issuing Houses. Might pick something up. Where can I get you?"

"Berebury Police Station."

Sloan collected Crosby and Sister Lucy from the Chapel. She accepted the money he offered her for the telephone call without embarrassment or demur. "Thank you, Inspector. Bills are quite a problem."

All three of them went back to the Parlor.

"It would seem, Mother," said Sister Lucy carefully, "that Sister Anne brought no dowry with her when she came. The Bursar's accounts for that year show no receipt that is likely to be hers."

"Thank you, Sister."

"I have had her will read to me over the telephone," went on Sister Lucy. "It was made at our Mother House the year she took her vows. It bequeaths all of that of which she died possessed to our Order."

"How much is likely to be involved?" asked Sloan casually.

Sister Lucy looked at him. "As far as I am aware, nothing at all. Sister Anne brought nothing with her and had no income of any sort while she was here."

Father MacAuley coughed. "Aren't we forgetting the potential?"

"What potential?" asked the Mother Prioress.

"Cartwright's Consolidated Carbons. That right, Inspector?"

"That's right, Father. I don't know where you get your information."

"You don't live in Strelitz Square on twopence ha'penny a week."

The Mother Prioress leaned forward enquiringly. "Had Sister Anne something to do with—er—Cartwright's Consolidated Carbons?"

"She did, marm. They are a chemical company formed by her uncle and father to exploit an invention of theirs of a method of combining carbon with various compounds for industrial chemists."

"I see." The Mother Prioress nodded. "That presumably was the source of the family income?"

"Yes, marm. You didn't know?"

"Not personally. My predecessor might have been told by Sister Anne. I do not think," she added gently, "that it would have concerned us in any way."

"Yes," interrupted Sister Gertrude unexpectedly. "Yes, it would, Mother."

Suddenly finding herself the object of every eye in the Parlor, Sister Gertrude blushed and lowered her head.

"Pray explain, Sister."

"This potential that you are talking about was some money that Sister Anne was to come into, wasn't it?"

Sloan nodded.

"Well, she knew about it. She told Sister Damien that the Convent would have it one day and then we could have our cloister."

There was silence.

Sister Gertrude looked from Inspector Sloan to Father Benedict MacAuley and back again. "I don't know if there would have been enough for a cloister or not," she said nervously, "but Sister Damien thought so, and so did Sister Anne."

"I think," said the Mother Prioress heavily, "that we had better see Sister Damien and Sister Michael now."

Sister Damien came first. Tall, thin and stiff-looking even in the soft folds of her habit, she swept the assembled company with a swift look and bowed to the Mother Prioress.

"The inspector has some questions for you, Sister. Pray answer them to the best of your recollection."

Sister Damien turned an expectant glance to Sloan.

"I want you to take your mind back to the events of Wednesday evening," he began easily. "Supper, for instance—what did you have?"

"Steak and kidney pie, and bread and butter pudding. The reading was of the martyrdom of Saint Denise."

"And Sister Anne sat next to you?"

"Naturally."

"Did you speak to her then?"

"Talking at meals is not permitted."

There was an irritating glint of self-righteousness in her eye that Sloan would dearly love to have squashed. Instead he said, "When did you see her again?"

"Not until Vespers."

"What about Recreation?"

"I didn't see her then. I was talking to Sister Jerome about some lettering ink for prayer cards. We are," she added insufferably, "permitted to move about at Recreation."

"When did you go into the Chapel?"

"About a quarter past eight."

"Was Sister Anne there then?"

"No. She came much later. I thought she was going to be late."

"But she wasn't?"

"No, not quite."

"Did you speak to her?" asked Sloan—and wished he hadn't.

"Speaking in Chapel is not permitted," said Sister Damien inevitably.

"Did you notice anything about her particularly?"

"No, Inspector, but we practice custody of the eyes."

"Custody of the eyes?"

The Mother Prioress leaned forward. "You could call it the opposite of observation. It is the only way to acquire the true concentration of the religious."

Sloan took a deep breath. Custody of the eyes didn't help him one little bit. "I see."

"There was just one thing, Inspector. ..."

"Well?"

"I think she may have been starting a cold. She did blow her nose several times."

"About the cloister. ..."

An entirely different sort of gleam came into Sister Damien's eye. She smoothed away an invisible crease in her gown.

"Yes, Inspector, we shall be able to have that now. Sister Anne said that when she was dead we should have enough money to have our cloister. She told me so several times. And there would be some for the missions, too. She took a great interest in missionary work."

"Did she tell you where the money was to come from?" asked Sloan.

"No. Just that it would be going back to those from whom it had been taken." Sister Damien seemed able to invest every remark she made with sanctimoniousness. "And that then restitution would have been made."

Sister Michael was fat and breathless and older. She did not hear at all well. Panting a little she agreed that Sister Anne had been very nearly late. The last in the Chapel, she thought. She hadn't noticed anything out of the ordinary but then she never did. She was a little deaf, you see, and had to concentrate hard on the service to make up for it.

But Sister Anne was there?

Sister Michael looked blank and panted a little more. One service was very like the next, Inspector, but she thought she would have remembered if Sister Anne hadn't been there, if he knew what she meant.

But she had just told him that Sister Anne was late.

Yes, well, Sister Damien had reminded her about that this morning.

What about yesterday morning when Sister Anne definitely wasn't there. Had she noticed then?

Well, actually, no. She wasn't ever very good in the mornings. It took her a little while to get going if he knew what she meant. Deafness, though she knew these minor disabilities were sent purely to test the weak on earth and were as nothing compared with the sufferings of saints and martyrs, was in fact very trying and led to a feeling of cut-offness. Of course, in some ways it made it easier to be properly recollected, if he knew what she meant.

He didn't. He gave up.

CHAPTER TEN

Harold Cartwright received them in his bedroom at The Bull. He appeared to have been working hard. The table was strewn with papers and there were more on the bed. There was a live tape recorder on the dressing table and he was talking into it when the two policemen arrived. He switched it off immediately.

"Sit down, gentlemen." He cleared two chairs. "It's not very comfortable but it's the best Cullingoak has to offer. I don't think they have many visitors at The Bull."

"Thank you, sir." Sloan took out a notebook. "We're just checking up on a matter of timing and would like to run through your movements on Wednesday again."

Cartwright looked at him sharply. "As I told you before, I drove myself down here from London. ..."

"When exactly did you leave?"

"I don't know exactly. About half past four. I wanted to miss the rush-hour traffic."

"Can anyone confirm the time you left?"

"I expect so," he said impatiently. "My secretary, for one. And my deputy director. I was in conference most of the afternoon and left as soon as I'd cleared up the matters arising from it. Is it important?"

"And how long did it take you to arrive here?"

He grimaced. "Longer than I thought it would. Several hundred other motorists had the same idea about leaving London before the rush hour. I drove into The Bull yard a few minutes before half past seven."

"Three hours? That's a long time."

"There was a lot of traffic."

"Even so ..."

"And I didn't know the way."

"Ah," said Sloan smoothly. "There is that. Did you by any chance take a wrong turning?"

"No," said Cartwright shortly. "I did not. But I was in no hurry. I had planned to have the evening to myself and most of the following day. I don't know enough about the routine of convents to know the best time to call on them—but in the event that didn't matter, did it?"

"This business that you had come all this way to talk to your cousin about, sir, you wouldn't care to tell me what it was?"

"No, Inspector," he said decisively. "I should not. I cannot conceive of it having any bearing on her death. It was a family affair."

"But you're staying on?"

"Yes, Inspector, I'm staying on." He sat quite still, a figure not without dignity even in an hotel bedroom. "The Mother Prioress has given me permission to attend Josephine's funeral but not—as you might have thought—to pay for it. Apparently a nun's burial is a very simple affair."

Superintendent Leeyes was unsympathetic. "You've had over twenty-four hours already, Sloan. The probability that a crime will be solved diminishes in direct proportion to the time that elapses afterwards, not as you might think in an inverse ratio."

"No, sir." Was that from "Mathematics for the Average Adult" or "Logic"?

"And Dabbe says that she died before seven and these women say they saw her after eight-thirty?"

"Just one woman says so, sir."

"What about the other fifty then?"

"They'd got their heads down. Sister Anne sat in the back row always and apparently it isn't done to look up or around. Custody of the eyes, they call it."

Leeyes growled. "And this woman that did see her then, what was she doing? Peeping between her fingers?"

"She could be lying," said Sloan cautiously. "I'm not sure. She could be crackers if it came to that."

"They can't any of them be completely normal, now can they?" retorted Leeyes robustly. "Asking to be locked up for life like that. It isn't natural."

"No, sir, but if there had been someone—not Sister Anne—at Vespers it would explain the glasses, wouldn't it?"

"It's better than 'Sister Anne Walks Again' which is what I thought you were going to say."

"No, sir, I don't believe in ghosts."

"Neither do I, Sloan," snapped Leeyes. "I may be practically senile, too, but I don't see how it explains the glasses either."

"Disguise," said Sloan. For one wild moment he contemplated asking the superintendent to cover his head with a large handkerchief to see if he would pass for a nun, but then he thought better of it. His pension was more important. "I reckon, sir, that either there wasn't anyone at all in Sister Anne's stall at Vespers or else it was someone there in disguise."

"Well done," said Leeyes nastily. "You should come with me on Mondays, Sloan. Learn a bit about Logic. And was it Cousin Harold who was standing there?"

"I don't know, sir."

"If it was, why the devil didn't he clear off? We didn't know he was there. We might never have found out."

"Those footprints aren't his."

"You're not making much headway, Sloan, are you?"

"Not since I've heard from Dr. Dabbe, sir."

For the first time he got some sympathy.

"It's usually the doctors," grumbled Superintendent Leeyes. "Try to pin them down on something and they'll qualify every single clause of every single sentence they utter. Then, when it's a blasted nuisance they'll be as dogmatic as … as …" he glared at his desk in his search for a comparative "… as a lady magistrate."

Sloan watched the superintendent drive off towards his home and next meal, and went back to his own room. Crosby was there with two large cups of tea and some sandwiches.

"Well, Crosby, what did you make of Sister Damien's story?"

"Someone wanted us to think Sister Anne was still alive at eight-thirty."

"Ah, yes, but was it Sister Damien who wanted us to think that? Or was it someone else?"

Crosby took a sandwich but offered no opinion.

"And *why* did they want us to think that?"

"Alibi?" suggested Crosby.

"Perhaps. No one missed Sister Anne at Recreation so presumably they can move about then more or less as they like."

"More or less, sir," echoed Crosby darkly.

Sloan grinned. The man had a sense of humor after all. "Did you give them back their keys?"

"Yes, sir. I went round all their cupboards with that Sister Lucy and opened them up. Nothing much there—food, stores and what have you. It was a hefty bunch of metal all right. Sister Lucy wears it round her waist all the time. They were certainly glad to have them back again."

"What about their local standing?"

"High, sir. I checked with quite a few people in the village. They like them. They aren't any trouble. Their credit is good and they pay on the nail for everything. They live carefully, not wasting anything, and they do as much of their shopping as possible in Cullingoak."

"That always goes down well."

"I got on to Dr. Carret, too. Only on the telephone though. He was out when I went there. He was called to the Convent when Sister Anne was found, realized she hadn't fallen downstairs in the ordinary way and sent for us."

"Very observant of him, that was. Is your standing with the canteen manageress good enough for another couple of cups?"

Apparently it was, for Crosby brought two refills back within minutes.

Sloan picked up a pencil. "Now, Crosby, where are we now?"

"Well, sir, yesterday we had this body that we thought had been murdered. Today we know it has been. Weapon, something hard but blunt, probably touched by Sister Peter early yesterday morning."

"And still to be found."

"Yes, sir. We know that Sister Anne was also Josephine Mary Cartwright and that her mother said 'Never darken these doors again' a long time ago. And that when her mother dies she was due to come into a lot of money."

"Only if she outlived her, Crosby. If she died first it reverts to Uncle Joe and his heirs, one of whom is camping at The Bull for some reason not yet revealed to us."

"Well, there's money for someone in it somewhere, sir."

"Show me the case where there isn't, Crosby, and I may not know how to solve it."

"Sir, did that thin one, Damien, know that if Sister Anne died before her uncle, the uncle got the lot?"

Sloan nodded approvingly. "That is something I should dearly like to know myself. You realize we have only got her word for it that Sister Anne—or someone she thought was Sister Anne—was at Vespers at eight-thirty? The other one—Sister Michael—what she said wasn't evidence. More like hearsay."

Crosby stopped, his cup half way to his lips. "You mean Sister Damien might be lying about that?" It was clearly a new idea to him.

"Don't look so shocked, Crosby."

"I didn't think *they* would lie, sir."

"Someone, somewhere," he said sarcastically, "is being untruthful with us, don't you think?"

"Oh, yes, sir, but I didn't think nuns would lie."

"Not quite cricket, Crosby?"

"Yes, sir—I mean—no, sir." Until he joined the Police Force, Crosby's ethics had been of a Sunday School variety—"speak the truth and shame the devil."

"If," went on Sloan, "Damien knew only that the Convent was to come into a lot of money when Sister Anne died—or thought that was so, she could just have thought she was doing the Convent a good turn—and Sister Anne, too if it came to that—by hurrying things along." He finished his tea and said profoundly: "Who can tell what people will do if they are cooped up together like that for year upon year without any sort of outlet? What *do* you do, Crosby, when you start getting on each other's nerves? Say a few more prayers?"

"I saw a film about a prisoner-of-war camp once," volunteered Crosby helpfully, "where they killed a chap because he sniffed."

Three loud knocks on the table at the end of a meal by the Mother Prioress indicated that she wished to speak to the Community. Half a hundred female faces turned attentively towards the Abbatial chair. There were round faces, oval faces, faces of the shape known outside the Convent (but never, never inside) as Madonna-type, fat faces, thin faces.

There were as many faces looking expectantly at the Reverend Mother as there were types of woman—almost—from the neat face of Sister Ignatius to the cheerful visage of Sister Hilda; from the calm features of Sister Jerome to the composed efficiency of Sister Radigund, the Infirmarium; from the still anxious look of Sister Peter to the intense concentration of Sister Damien.

"My daughters …" The Mother Prioress surveyed the dim Refectory. It was long since dark outside, and the mock electric candles in their sconces on the wall provided only the minimum of light. "My daughters, through the centuries those of our Order have gone through many trials and tribulations, compared with which our present discomforts are as nothing. What we now endure is unfamiliar and distasteful to us—intrusion and enquiry are an anathema to the religious life—but it is not for us to complain now or at any time of what we suffer." Her gaze traveled down the ranks of nuns. "When we renounced the world we did not automatically leave doubt and sorrow behind. Nor are we immune from the physical laws of cause and effect. Nor should we wish to be."

One of the novices, she who was sitting nearest to the pepperpot, sneezed suddenly. The Novice-Mistress leaned forward slightly to identify the culprit.

"Sister Anne," went on the Mother Prioress unperturbed, "died on Wednesday evening some time after supper, probably in the corridor leading from the Great Hall to the kitchens. Her body was put into the broom cupboard and later thrown down the cellar steps. As you know, she was found there after a search on Thursday morning. It is now Friday evening. I should like you all to go back in your minds to Wednesday evening and consider if you saw or heard anything out of the ordinary pattern of religious behavior." She did not pause here as she might have done but went straight on to say, "On Thursday evening, Guy Fawkes' Night, the effigy of a nun was burnt on the bonfire lit by the students of the Agricultural Institute. In the ordinary course of events I should not have troubled the Community with this information, believing that the incident was more in the nature of high spirits than bigotry, but the guy was dressed in the habit that normally hangs behind the door of the garden room."

It was evident that this was news to some of the nuns.

"Moreover, the guy was wearing Sister Anne's glasses."

This was a bombshell. Heads went up. Grave glances were exchanged between the older Sisters. The younger ones looked excited or frightened, according to temperament.

"You will not, therefore, be surprised to know that the police require to know the exact whereabouts of every Sister from suppertime on Wednesday until they retired to their cells. If you spoke to Sister Anne after supper, or if you have any other information, it should be communicated to me, and only to me. I shall be in the Parlor until Vespers." She paused. "The police also wish to be told the secular name of every member of the Community, the date of her profession, and the address from which she came to the Convent of St. Anselm."

The dining room at the Agricultural Institute was also known as the

Refectory, but there the resemblance ended. It was brightly lit and very noisy indeed. One hundred and fifty healthy young men were just coming to the end of a substantial meal. Fourteen staff were having theirs at the High Table on a dais at one end of the long room. Sundry maids were rattling dirty dishes through a hatch into the kitchen, and making it quite clear that they thought any meal which began at seven-fifteen should end by eight o'clock.

Marwin Ranby, sitting in the centre of the High Table, let the maids finish before he stood up. Students were easy to come by, maids much more difficult.

"Gentlemen, in its short life this Institute has acquired a reputation for outrage on the night that commemorates the failure of the Gunpowder Plot. ..."

There were several cheers.

"Usually the damage can be repaired by the use of one simple commodity. Money."

More cheers.

"And apologies, of course."

"Good old Mr. Ranby, sir," called out a wit.

Ranby gave a thin smile. "Well, it isn't good old anyone this time. Granted, in the ordinary run of events, we might have got by with a handsome apology to the Mother Prioress and an even more handsome contribution to the Convent funds. ..."

Loud groans.

"This time it's much more serious. ..."

More groans.

"Yesterday, as you know full well, was November the Fifth. The evening before that—Wednesday—a nun died in the Convent. The police, who, as you know, performed an excellent rescue job on the guy ..."

Loud laughter, interspersed with more groans.

"The police," said Ranby firmly, "tell me that that habit came from the Convent, probably the same day the nun died. Now, they're not accusing anyone of being implicated in this death but they do need to know who it was who was in the Convent, how they got in and when. I think you can all understand that." He looked quickly from face to face. "Now, I'm asking those responsible—however many of you there are with a hand in this—to come to my study at nine o'clock tonight."

CHAPTER ELEVEN

Celia Faine was in the Principal's study with Marwin Ranby when Sloan and Crosby arrived. A maid had just deposited a tray of coffee on the table.

"Come in, Inspector, come in. How's the chase going?"

"Warming up nicely, sir, thank you."

Ranby eyed him thoughtfully. "I'm glad to hear it. I've got good news for you, too. We've got the culprits who made the guy." He turned. "Celia, my dear, will you be hostess while I tell the Inspector about Tewn and the others?"

Celia Faine smiled and took up the coffee pot. "Don't be too hard on them, will you? They're nice lads and I'm sure they meant no harm."

Ranby frowned. "No, I don't think they did, but you can't be too sure. William Tewn is the chap you're looking for, Inspector. As far as I can make out, three of them initiated the scheme—a third-year man called Parker, and Tewn and Bullen, who are second year. Parker's the cleverest of the three—clever enough to organize the expedition without going to any risk himself, I should say. Bullen and Tewn went over the fence into the Convent property on Wednesday night, while Parker kept watch. Bullen went as far as the outside wall, and Tewn went inside the building. He came out with the habit."

"One moment, sir. How did you discover this?"

He gave a wry laugh. "They—er—gave themselves up so to speak, in response to my appeal after supper this evening. I've just been speaking to them and they're waiting in my secretary's room for you."

"Sugar?" Celia Faine handed round the coffee cups expertly. Sloan saw she would be a great asset to the rather too-efficient Principal. "Tell

90

me, Inspector, where do you think they kept the guy until Thursday evening?"

"I know the answer to that one," said Marwin Ranby rather shortly. "In one of the cowsheds. That's where they made it up from the straw and the old sack. They had their firewood all ready. I hadn't raised any objection to a straightforward bonfire, you see ..."

"No one thinks it's your fault, dear," she said soothingly.

"Nevertheless," went on Ranby, more philosophically, "I suppose I should have thought something like this might happen ... all the same, I don't like it. What I would like, Inspector, are those three men over at the Convent first thing in the morning to apologize in person to the Mother Prioress and the Community. It's the very least we can do. ..."

"Certainly, sir," agreed Sloan peaceably. Ranby had good reason for wanting to keep on the right side of the Reverend Mother. "If you want it that way. I don't see that it can do any harm."

But once again he was wrong.

Messrs. Parker, Bullen and Town were not too dismayed to find Sloan and Crosby taking an interest in their escapade.

"Just our bad luck that we chose a night when one of the nuns goes and gets herself killed," grumbled Parker. "Otherwise we stood a good chance of getting away with it."

"You must admit it was a good joke, Inspector." Town was a fresh-faced boy with curly hair and a few remaining infant freckles. "Especially with old Namby-Pam ... with the Principal going to be married at the Convent at the end of the month. Sort of appropriate."

It was a long, long time since Sloan's idea of a good joke had been anything so primitive.

"And?" he said dispassionately.

"Well," said Town, "it was a piece of cake, wasn't it?"

The other two nodded. Bullen, a slow-speaking, well-built boy, said, "No trouble at all."

"Come on then," snapped Sloan. "How did you go about it? Ring the front door bell and ask for a spare habit?"

"No, we went to the back door," said Town promptly. "At least to the sort of cellar door."

"And just opened it, I suppose. Without knocking."

"Yes," agreed Town blandly. "Yes, that was exactly what we did."

"At what time was this excursion?"

"About half past nine on Wednesday evening."

"And you expect me to believe that this door was unlocked?"

"Oh, yes," said Tewn. "I just put my hand on the door and it opened."

"And the habit?"

"That was there."

"Waiting for you?"

Tewn's freckles colored up. "That's right."

"And you just picked it up and came out again?"

"That's right." Tewn poked a finger at Bullen. "I was only inside half a minute, wasn't I?"

"Less if anything," said Bullen. "Like I said—no trouble at all."

"No trouble!" echoed an exasperated Sloan. "That's where you're wrong. There's lots of trouble."

"But if Tewn was only inside half a minute and Bullen confirms it," said the third young man, "they can't have had anything to do with this nun, can they?"

Sloan turned towards him. "You're Parker, I suppose? Well, there's just one flaw in your reasoning. How do I know that they're not both lying? Suppose you tell me where you were at the time?"

"Here in the Institute," said Parker.

"In the Biology lab, I suppose."

Parker flushed. "Yes, as it happens I was."

"Any witnesses to prove it?"

"No ... no. I don't think anyone saw me there."

"Well, then ..." Sloan let the sentence hang unfinished while he surveyed the three of them. "So you three arranged the snaffling of the habit, did you? And you carried out the operation according to plan without any sort of hitch?"

"That's right," said Tewn. "We never saw a soul."

"When you got the habit, what next?"

"Bullen and I brought it back with us. I kept it in my room until yesterday morning and then we made it up into a guy. It was easy," said Tewn ingenuously, "because nuns don't have much of a figure, do they?"

"And the glasses," put in Sloan casually. "Where did you pick them up?"

"What glasses?" asked Tewn.

"The guy that I rescued was wearing glasses," said Sloan impatiently. "Where did they come from?"

Parker nodded. "Yes, it was. They were on her—it, I mean—when Bullen and I carried it out to the fire."

"I didn't see any glasses," said Town. "We put a couple of buttons in for eyes."

Bullen stirred. "She was wearing glasses when Parker and I went to fetch her for the fire. We thought you'd put them on her, Town—they looked proper old-fashioned."

"Not me," said Town. "I didn't go back to the cowshed at all after we'd made her up in the morning. I was on the pig rota, remember? We had a farrowing at half past six and I jolly nearly missed my supper."

"I thought you'd cadged an old pair from Matron," said Parker. "She wears them just like that."

Ranby was right: Parker was the most intelligent of the three. Sloan said, "So you didn't take them from the Convent with the habit?"

"Oh, no," said Town quickly. "Besides we wouldn't have known they weren't wanted, would we?"

"Like you knew the habit wasn't wanted?" suggested Sloan smoothly. "Like you knew the door would be open for you …"

Town's color flared up again, Parker looked sullen, Bullen quite impassive. All three remained silent.

"If, by any chance, any one of the three of you remembers how it came about that that cellar door was to be open to you on Wednesday evening, and that an old habit that nobody wanted just happened to be lying there for the taking, perhaps you'd be kind enough to let me know. It might, incidentally, just be in your own interests to do so, if you get me."

Sloan and Crosby went back to the study. Celia Faine was sitting by the fire. She smiled at him. "Here's the inspector again. How did you find Marwin's little criminals?"

"Guilty, I hope," said Ranby. "I don't think there was any doubt, was there, that they got that habit?"

"None at all, sir. They admitted it."

"Their idea of a good lark, I suppose."

"That's right, sir, but they say they didn't take the glasses—the ones that the guy was wearing, remember?"

"Yes, Inspector, I remember. I'm not ever likely to forget, but I don't know who can help you there."

"You can."

"Me?" Ranby looked quite startled. "How?"

"By telling me who could have had access to your cowsheds during the day."

"Cowsheds?" His brow cleared. "The guy—of course. Why, anyone, I suppose. There are all those who go in at milking and to clean and those who teach on milk handling and the Milk Marketing Board people. Any number in one day."

"The sheds are never locked?"

"I doubt if there's even a key," said Ranby. "There's nothing to steal, you see."

"So anyone could go in there at any time of the day without it occasioning any interest?"

"Anyone from the Institute, of course. I don't know about outsiders. The vet's here often enough, and odd Inspectors—Ministry ones, I mean."

"I see, sir. Thank you. I think that's all I need to know for the present. Goodnight, miss, goodnight, sir—sorry to have to disturb you so late. ..." At the door, he turned and looked back. "These students of yours—are they allowed out into the village at all?"

"Oh, yes, Inspector, but they must be in by nine on a weekday and half past ten at the weekend. That's early, I know, but we have an early start here. If they're going to be dairy farmers they might as well get used to it now, that's the way we look at it."

Hobbett lived in a depressed-looking cottage just off Cullingoak High Street. Neither he nor his wife were noticeably welcoming to Sloan and Crosby. They were led through into the kitchen. It was not clean. A pile of dirty dishes had been taken as far as the sink but not washed. Parts of both an old loaf and a new one lay on the table with some more dirty cups. There were two chairs by the kitchen grate. Mrs. Hobbett subsided into one of these which immediately demonstrated itself to be a rocking chair. She went backwards and forwards, never taking her eyes off the two policemen.

"Just a few more questions, Hobbett," said Sloan mildly.

"Well?"

"We're interested in this key of yours to the Convent."

"What about it?"

"Where do you keep it for a start?"

Hobbett jerked his thumb over towards the back door. "There, on a hook."

"Is it there now?"

"You've got eyes, haven't you? That's it, all right."

"Is it always there?"

"Except when it's in my pocket."

"You never lend it to anyone?"

"Me? What for? Catch people wanting to go in one of them places? Never. And it's my opinion that some of them that's inside would a lot rather be outside."

"Nevertheless, you always lock up before you go every night?"

Hobbett scowled. "Yes, I do, mate. Every night, like I said."

Sloan was quite silent on the way back to Berebury, and Crosby couldn't decide whether he was brooding or dozing.

"Hobbett's the best bet," said Sloan suddenly.

Brooding, after all. "Yes, sir."

"He could have got into that garden room without it seeming odd and taken the habit down to the cellar. Then all he has to do is to leave the door unlocked when he goes home."

"Doesn't that dragon at the gate—"

"Polycarp."

"Doesn't she check up on that door?"

"No need, Crosby. The door from the cellar to the Convent proper is always kept locked. The Reverend Mother said so."

"Why didn't he just take the habit, then?"

"Him? Catch him doing anything that'll lose him that nice soft number of a job he's got? Don't be daft. Look at it this way. All he has to do is to shift an old habit from that garden room—or whatever you call it—to his little lobby place. Nothing criminal in that."

"Then give the key to those lads?"

"Give nothing, man. He just forgets to lock the door, that's all. Nothing criminal in that, either. 'Ever so sorry, Sister. It must have slipped my mind. Won't happen again.' That's if they ever get to know, which they stood a good chance of not doing. Besides, that way Tewn, Parker and Whatshisname—"

"Bullen."

"—Bullen have all the fun of going inside themselves. Much more daring, blast them. Heroes, that's probably what they think they are. Brave men. They've been inside a Convent. Something to tell their grandchildren about. I wonder what Hobbett got out of it?"

"A few drinks?" suggested Crosby.

"And," said Sloan, still pursuing his own train of thought, "he didn't think he would be doing any harm because he knew they couldn't get any further."

"Because the cellar door was always kept locked," supplied Crosby. "I say, sir, that's a point, isn't it? I mean, who opened the cellar door in the first place?"

Sloan grunted. "We might make a detective out of you yet, Crosby. Who do you think opened it?"

Crosby subsided. "I don't know, sir."

"Neither do I," retorted Sloan briefly. "The important thing is that it was opened from the inside."

"That narrows the field a bit, sir, doesn't it?"

"Does it, Crosby?"

"Well, you couldn't have just anybody walking about inside, could you?"

"No."

"Well, then, sir. ..."

"You're forgetting Caesar's wife, Crosby."

Crosby doubled-declutched to give himself time to think. "Who, sir?"

"Caesar's wife. She was above suspicion."

CHAPTER TWELVE

In the beginning Saturday morning resolved itself into routine.

Harold Cartwright had a large mail delivered to him at The Bull, and spent many more than the usual three minutes on the telephone to London. Mrs. Briggs at the Cullingoak Post Office was hard put to it to keep up with his calls as well as serve her usual Saturday morning customers.

That part of the Agricultural Institute on early call got up and began to go about its business, regretting being born to the land and married to the land, wishing that it led urban lives when it wouldn't have had to get up early ever and not get up at all on Saturdays.

Life at the Convent proceeded very much as usual. Sister Gertrude woke the Community at the appointed time and they began to work their way through their immemorial, unchanging round. With one difference. Each Sister had to write on a piece of paper her secular name and address, date of profession and precise location immediately after supper on Wednesday evening. Only old Mother St. Thérèse, to whom all days were the same, found this difficult.

It was routine, too, at the Berebury Police Station to begin with. Superintendent Leeyes sent for Sloan as soon as he got to his office. He was at his worst in the morning. That, too, was routine.

"Seen the papers?" Leeyes indicated a truly sepulchral photograph of Sister Polycarp behind the grille, caught in the camera flash with her eyes shut and mouth open. Under this was a much more sophisticated picture taken from a long distance with a telephoto lens of the outside of the Convent through the trees. The effect was sinister in the extreme.

"Pursuing your enquiries, Sloan, that's what they say you're doing."

"Yes, sir." Sloan bent over to read the report. He was too good a policeman to scorn any facts newspaper reporters might dig out. Besides, they were free men by comparison—no Judges' Rules for them.

There wasn't very much in the paper. The brief news that a nun (unnamed) had died in the Convent of St. Anselm at Cullingoak (short historical note on the Order and its Foundress—see any reference book) once the family seat of the Faines (three paragraphs on the Faine family straight from the nearest Guide to the Landed Gentry), and what they were pleased to call a startling coincidence—the burning of a nun as a guy the very next night—at the nearby Agricultural Institute (run by the Calleshire County Council, Principal, M. Ranby, B.Sc., formerly Deputy Head of West Laming School). Mr. Ranby, said the report, was not available for comment at the Institute yesterday. "Wise man," thought Sloan. Then followed a highly circumstantial account of the burning of the guy by "a student" who preferred not to give his name. The story wound up with a few generalizations about student rags and the information that an inquest was to be held on Monday morning next in the Guildhall, Berebury. Sloan straightened up.

"Could be worse."

Leeyes grunted. He did not like the Press. "Wait till you've seen the Sundays. Especially if they get hold of this time business."

"Or the trio who got the habit. A pretty picture they would make. By the way, sir, it was Bullen and Tewn's footprints Crosby found. He's just checked. Bullen stood in one spot under the rhododendrons while Tewn went down in the cellar for the habit. That's what they told us, and the footprints tie up with that."

"Not Harold Cartwright's?"

"No, sir."

"Can't understand what the devil he's doing here, Sloan."

"I don't know what he's doing, but he's working," said Sloan. "I've got a man keeping an eye on him. Lots and lots of paper work, telephone calls, tape recorders, the lot."

"He'll be lucky if he gets anything done that way. I never do. Quiet thinking is what gets things done, Sloan. More things are wrought by—er—quiet thought than you would believe."

"Yes, sir."

"Logical thought, of course, Sloan."

"Of course, sir."

"There's one aspect of this case I've been thinking about a lot. …"

"Sir?"

"This weapon that Dabbe talks about. …"

Sloan nodded. "He said it was something smooth and round and heavy."

"That describes a paperweight *and* a cannon ball," said the superintendent testily. "We haven't found it yet, have we?"

"Not yet, sir." Sloan liked the "we." "We instituted a search on Thursday morning but found nothing. That Sister Peter wasn't what you could call a good witness. Too worked up for one thing. Swore she showed us everywhere she's been, and that wasn't very exciting, but no sign of any blunt instruments."

"It must have been there, Sloan."

"It must have been there when she touched it, sir. Crosby and I didn't see it. We went back for another look afterwards when she'd gone off to tell her troubles to somebody else, but we couldn't pick any lead up anywhere."

"Narrows the field a bit, doesn't it?" said Superintendent Leeyes, just as Crosby had done.

"I don't see why," said Sloan obstinately. "Someone had only to know what it—whatever it was—was there, hadn't they? Comes to the same thing."

Leeyes pounced. "Ah, so you think it's an outside job, do you?"

Sloan shook his head. "I don't know, sir. Not yet. I've an open mind."

"Have you?" Leeyes glared at him. "I hope that you don't mean an empty one."

"No, sir. On the contrary, the possibilities are still infinite."

The concept of infinity had already come up in the superintendent's Logic course. It was now a word he treated with respect and no longer understood. He let the inspector get as far as the door. "Sloan …"

"Sir?"

"Do you know what they make nuns' habits from?"

"Wool, I suppose, sir."

"Ah, but what sort of wool?"

"I couldn't say, sir."

"From black sheep, Sloan."

The day was still relatively young when Sloan and Crosby reached the

Convent. The Mother Superior and Sister Lucy received them as if it was already half over. The Mother Superior handed him a list of names.

"Thank you, marm. I feel we need all the information we can get in this matter."

"Such knowledge as I have is, of course, at your disposal, Inspector."

"First, marm, I have some news for you. Mr. Ranby has traced the culprits of Thursday night's incident—three of his students were responsible for making the guy. He intends to bring them over this morning to apologize in person."

She inclined her head graciously. "There is no need for him to go to such trouble, but if he wishes it. ... Has their escapade any bearing on Sister Anne's death, would you say?"

"If," countered Sloan carefully, "she had happened upon them in the grounds or in the Convent itself it might have—but I think it unlikely."

"So do I," said the Mother Superior firmly. "Sister Anne—God rest her soul—would have reported such intruders to me immediately. I do not like to think that the students would have reacted to discovery with murder."

"No, marm, nor do I."

They faced each other in the small Parlor. Irrelevantly it spun through Sloan's mind that he had never seen such fine skin on two women before. The older, more flaccid face of the Mother Superior reminded him of cream, the younger, firmer skin of Sister Lucy of the peaches that go with it. He remembered reading somewhere that good skin—like a good car— only needed washing with water. He must make a note to tell his wife about their complexions.

"Marm, there is a question that I must put to you."

"Yes, Inspector?"

"Do you have anyone here who would rather not be here?"

"I do not think so."

"No one who would—er—figuratively speaking, of course—like to leap over the wall?"

"No, Inspector. We are a Community here in the true sense. I do not think any Sister could reach a state of wanting to be released from her vows without the Community becoming aware of it. That is so, Sister Lucy, is it not?"

"Yes, Mother. It is something that cannot be hidden."

"Likes and dislikes?" put in Sloan quickly.

The Mother Superior smiled faintly. "Neither are permitted here."

"You realize, marm," he said more crisply, "that any—shall we say, disaffection—would be pertinent to my enquiry, and that my enquiry must go on until it determines how Sister Anne died."

She inclined her head. "Certainly, Inspector, but if we had any disaffected Sister here, or even one unable to subdue her own strong likes or dislikes, she would have been sent away. There are fewer locks in a Convent than the popular Press would have one believe."

Sloan looked up suddenly. "*Has* anyone left recently?"

"Yes, as it happens they have."

"Who?" He should have been told this before.

She looked at him. "I cannot see that the departure of a Sister from the Convent before the unhappy events of the past week can pertain to your enquiry."

"I must be the judge of that."

She gestured acquiescence. "Sister Lucy shall find her secular name for you. It was Sister Bertha."

"When did she leave?"

"About three weeks ago."

"Where did she go?"

"I do not know."

"You don't know?" echoed Sloan in spite of himself.

"It was not properly our concern to enquire," said the Mother Superior. "She felt that she could not continue in the religious life and asked to be released from her vows. This was done through the usual channels and she left."

"Just like that?" asked Sloan stupidly.

"Just like that, Inspector."

He pulled himself together. "Had she any special connection with Sister Anne? Was she a friend of hers, for instance?"

"Friendship is not permitted in a Convent. We are all Sisters here. She would have known Sister Anne to just the same extent as we all knew Sister Anne. No less and no more."

"And you knew she wanted to leave—as a Community, I mean?"

"Yes, we knew she wanted to leave."

"If, marm," he persisted, "Sister Anne had been in a similar frame of mind, do you think you would have known?"

"Yes, Inspector," she said with certainty. "You probably do not realize how close are the lives we lead here. Private life, in the usual sense, does not exist. One therefore becomes very aware of the thoughts, not to say the spiritual condition, of one's Sisters. It is inevitable, and often does not even require formulation into words. Sister Anne, I do assure you, was not contemplating renouncing her vows."

Sloan and Crosby went back to Berebury Police Station. Sloan spread out on his desk the list of names that the Reverend Mother had given him. They had barely sat down when the telephone beside Sloan rang.

"Yes. Speaking. Who?" It wasn't a local call.

"Jenkins," said a voice. "You rang me in London yesterday, remember? About a family called Cartwright. You still interested?"

"I am. Go on."

"I think you're on to something, Inspector. Cartwright's Consolidated Carbons have made a move."

"Have they?" asked Sloan cautiously. "What sort of a move?"

"Towards going public. It seems, and I think this will interest you—that they have had everything prepared for some time."

"Just waiting for someone to say the word?"

"So it would seem," said the London man. "These things take time, you know. Bankers to be instructed, brokers to be interested and so forth, to say nothing of organizing some useful advance publicity. Sounds as if they're going to chance their arm about the publicity buildup and go all out for speed. They'll get a good bit from the Sundays, of course. They'll be laying that on now."

"How much speed do they want?"

"According to my informant, and he's usually reliable," said Jenkins, "applications will open at ten o'clock next Thursday morning and close at one minute past. I don't know at what sort of figure but I dare say they'll be oversubscribed. They're a well-organized firm."

"You can say that again," said Sloan dryly.

"What's that? Oh, yes, I was forgetting your end."

"So they'll be a public company at one minute past ten next Thursday morning?"

"That's it. Provided they deposit the necessary Articles of Association, seals and what-have-you with the Registrar and comply with all the rules and regulations and keep up with their paperwork."

"Oh, they will," Sloan assured him. "They will. I don't think we need worry about that."

"Going to put in for some?" asked Jenkins.

"Some what?"

"Shares."

Sloan laughed. "I'm not a betting man."

"There's no risk," said the other seriously. "Cartwright's Consolidated Carbons must be one of the safest firms in the industry."

"I wasn't thinking about their carbons."

"No, no, of course not. There's just one thing, Inspector, though. If you've got any reservations about the company and the City gets to hear about them before Thursday it'll cost someone a great deal of money."

"And after Thursday?"

"It'll still cost a great deal of money but different people will lose."

"And that's business?"

"That's business, Inspector."

"I think I'll stick to police work."

"I should," agreed Jenkins. "Much cleaner."

Sloan put down the telephone. "Curiouser and curiouser, Crosby. That needs a bit of thinking about." He smoothed out the list of nuns for the second time. "Have you got the name of the one that got away?"

Crosby produced his notebook. "Miss Eileen Lome, no fixed address. "

"Surely ..."

"Last known address, then, sir."

"That's more like it."

"144, Frederick Street, Luston. Sister Bertha that was."

"We must see her, Crosby, just in case she can tell us anything."

"Yes, sir." The telephone rang again. Crosby answered it, and then handed over the receiver. "For you, sir, I think. I can't quite hear who it is—it's a bit faint like."

"Inspector Sloan here. Who is that?"

"The Convent of St. Anselm, Inspector. It's Sister Gertrude speaking. Can you come quickly, Inspector, please? It's Sister Ninian. She was walking through the shrubbery ..." the voice faded away.

"What happened to her?" asked Sloan urgently.

"Hallo, Inspector, are you there? This is Sister Gertrude from the Convent. It's about Sister Ninian ..."

"I heard that bit. What has happened to Sister Ninian?"

"Nothing, Inspector, not to her. To somebody else ..."

"What has happened?" shouted Sloan.

"Another accident," came the voice of Sister Gertrude distantly.

"Listen carefully, Sister. Keep the lower part of the telephone in front of your lips while you are talking and tell me who the accident has happened to."

The answer came so loudly that he jumped.

"We don't know who he is."

"He? You mean it's a man?"

"That's right, Inspector. He's dead in the shrubbery as I said. Sister Ninian found him."

"This is very important, Sister. What sort of a man? Can you describe him?"

"Oh, yes, Inspector, easily. Young, with curly hair, oh—and a few freckles. Do you know him?"

Sloan groaned aloud.

CHAPTER 13

It was a subdued Polycarp who opened the grille and then the Parlor door, and a white and slightly shaking Sister Lucy who greeted them there. A young, silent Sister was with her.

"Mother said to take you straight to the shrubbery, Inspector, as soon as you arrived." The religious decorum was still there but it was wavering a little in the interests of speed. "It's quickest if you come through the house and out through the garden room."

She led the way through the building, past the magnificent staircase, down the dim corridor where Sister Anne had died and through a door into the room of the flower vases.

She turned a drawn face to him. "We don't know what happened at all, Inspector. Or when."

He nodded without slackening his pace.

"You probably haven't met Sister Ninian, Inspector. She's one of our older Sisters. She is very fond of gardening and she often takes a turn through the grounds to keep an eye on things. She was just walking along this path when she turned down here."

"Down here" turned out to be a narrow path running round the perimeter of the Convent grounds. Sloan caught sight of black-habited figures among the bare winter trees. They were clustered round a still form lying awkwardly half in and half out of some bushes.

The Mother Superior turned when she heard him.

"I fear he's quite dead, Inspector."

Sloan stepped beside her and looked down. There was no doubt about him being dead. The freckles that Sister Gertrude had described must have been those on his arms. She couldn't have seen them on his face. It was suffused with blood, a terrible, mottled red and blue. A bloated tongue stuck out between lips parted in the mocking rictus of death.

"Strangulation," he said briefly.

"Inspector. ..." It seemed suddenly as if it was a great effort for her to speak. "Could this be William Tewn?"

"What makes you say that, marm? Have you ever seen this boy before?"

"No. No, never. Mr. Ranby came to see me this morning after you had gone. He brought two boys with him to apologize for the guy but he had been going to bring three. He said they couldn't find William Tewn." She stared at the supine figure. "He said he would send him over on his own whenever he turned up."

Looking down at the dead youth, Sloan felt suddenly old and tired. "Yes, marm, this is William Tewn. Now, could you all move away from here without disturbing the ground, please. It's very important. ..."

There was quite a gathering of nuns—Sister Gertrude, Sister Lucy, and three or four whom he did not know. He shepherded them gently back to the main path and left Crosby to rope off the area round the body.

"Now, if someone would tell me what happened. ..."

The story was Sister Ninian's to begin with. She was a neat, sensible woman of about sixty, and economical of speech. "In winter, when it is fine, we all take some exercise before our midday meal. I do some of the gardening and make a practice of walking in a slightly different route each day. That way I can see things needing doing before they get out of hand. This path, as you can see, Inspector, runs round the entire Convent property. The Agricultural Institute is the other side of that field. Cows have been known to stray, and the branches of trees to fall. That is the sort of thing I keep my eyes open for."

Sloan nodded. Not, of course, for the bodies of dead man. That was chance.

"I had just turned down this portion of the path when I noticed a shoe sticking out. ..."

It was surprising, thought Sloan academically, how often it was a shoe that caught the attention. The soles of a pair of shoes were conspicuous in a horticultural setting.

"I approached it and found the body. I came back along this path until I found two other Sisters—Sister Gertrude and Sister Hilda here. They came back with me to the spot, and then Sister Gertrude went back to the Convent to tell Mother."

"And I," said the Mother Superior, taking up the tale, "asked Sister Gertrude to send for you while I came out here to see myself."

"Bringing Sister Lucy with you?" asked Sloan suddenly.

She looked at him curiously. "No, Inspector, as it happened I did not bring Sister Lucy out here with me. I left her waiting in the Parlor to bring you here as soon as you arrived. Sister Gertrude came out here with the news that she had caught you at the Police Station and that you were on your way. We were exceedingly relieved to hear it."

Sister Lucy, then, had been white and shaking without having seen the body? He cast back in his mind to Thursday morning. She hadn't reacted like that to the body of Sister Anne.

"Mr. Ranby and the two students could scarcely have got back to the Institute," said the Mother Superior, "before Sister Gertrude came in."

Sloan looked at his watch. "Were they with you long?"

"No. The two young men said they were very sorry for their intrusion; Mr. Ranby apologized on behalf of the Institute and then they went. I had had to keep them waiting a few moments because of Mr. Cartwright."

"He was here, too, this morning?"

"Yes, Inspector, he and Father MacAuley both came to see me after you left."

Sloan sighed. "I think we had all better go indoors, marm, and Crosby can take this all down. Besides, Dr. Dabbe will be here again in a minute or two."

"What?" howled Superintendent Leeyes. "I don't believe it."

"He's dead," said Sloan flatly. "Strangled and dragged off the path and half under some bushes."

It seemed to Sloan that he had spent most of the last three days standing in the dark, drafty corridor where the Convent kept their telephone.

"Tewn? Tewn?" said the superintendent. "That's the one of the three that actually went inside the Convent for the habit, isn't it?"

"That's right, sir."

Leeyes used an expression that would have surprised the watch committee.

"Yes, sir." Sloan endorsed the sentiment watch committee or no.

"It would have to be him."

"Yes, sir." Bitterly. "It would."

"How far did you get with him last night?"

"Just that it was child's play to walk in the cellar door and pick up the habit. No trouble they said."

"He must have seen something," said Leeyes.

"Yes, sir."

"No hint of what it could have been when you spoke to him last night?"

"Not a clue, sir. I'm pretty sure that these three arranged with Hobbett— he's the handyman there—to leave the cellar door unlocked that night and the old habit inside. I don't see any other possibility—there was no sign of forced entry. And it sounded as if everything went according to plan. Parker kept watch on their return to the Institute, Bullen guarded the cellar door and line of retreat and Town went inside."

"And so he dies."

"Yes, sir."

"Nasty, Sloan. I don't like it. Though tell me this—if he's going to be killed, why wait until today? It's Saturday now, it was Wednesday when they went into the Convent …"

Sloan thought quickly. "I didn't know who he was until after nine o'clock last night. Someone else might not have known either …"

"That's true. Sitting waiting for him to be identified, and then, when he is, killing him."

"It would have been dark in that cellar on Wednesday night," conceded Sloan. "No one could have recognized him."

"What about today?" asked the superintendent heavily.

"I've only seen the Mother Superior so far. And the Sisters who were with the body when I got here. She says that the Principal had arranged for all three students to come across with him to say they were sorry for Wednesday's escapade but that Town just didn't turn up. Ranby was a bit put out apparently and said he would send Town over on his own later."

"No wonder he didn't come."

"Yes, sir. I'm going straight round there as soon as I've seen Dr. Dabbe. I'm going to need all the information he can give me. …"

It wasn't a great deal.

Sloan stood beside the pathologist out in the shrubbery.

"Strangulation," agreed Dabbe. "Not manual. I think it's a bit of fuse wire but I can't be sure. The skin's too engorged. Over your head in a flash, a quick jerk and that's that."

"Vicious."

"Neat and clean," said Dabbe. "And certain. Quiet, too. No time for a shout, you see. Not that there's anyone to hear out here, is there?"

They looked round the silent grounds.

"Convent, that way," said Sloan. "The Institute, the other. Neither in earshot."

"No nuns about at the time?"

"They're not let out until twelve. For their constitutional. There's Hobbett, their gardening factotum. He would have been out in the grounds somewhere …"

That wasn't the pathologist's concern and he was soon back with the body.

"Killed on this path, would you say, and dragged into the bushes by the armpits? You can still see where the jacket has been pulled up. His heels made a couple of scuff marks, too."

Sloan peered down at the last pathetic imprints made by one William Tewn, student.

"A good place really," went on the pathologist. "He only had to be pulled a yard or two and he's practically invisible in all this growth. And whoever did it remembered to stand on that dead wood. Doubt if you'll find a footprint there, and the path's too hard."

"Crosby's tried," said Sloan, "and he couldn't pick up anything. When did it all happen?"

The pathologist looked at his watch. "Not more than two hours ago—say three at the very outside …"

"After half past nine then …"

"And not less than an hour ago—an hour and a half more likely."

"It's not half past twelve yet. That would make the outside limits somewhere between half past nine and half past eleven, only he wasn't available just after eleven when the Institute party set out, so that makes it earlier than eleven, doesn't it?"

But abstract speculation wasn't of interest to the pathologist either. Of all men his work was to do with fact, with demonstrable fact.

"Perhaps I'll be able to narrow it down for you later," he said cautiously.

Sloan nodded and asked the question on which everything hung. "Any clue—any clue at all as to who could have done it?"

Dr. Dabbe considered the body. "He's not very big, is he? Anyone could have dragged him that short distance. As for whipping a length of fuse wire round someone's neck—that's not strength so much as strategy. You could only do it at all if it was totally unexpected. If you were to insist on some indication as to the person who could have done it ..." Sloan remained silent, which was as good as insisting. "... then all I could tell you with any certainty," offered the pathologist, "was that they were probably as tall or taller than Tewn—and you could work that out for yourself. I can't tell you if it was a man or a woman but I can tell you that it wouldn't have been impossible for a woman—especially a tallish one. A quick flick of the wrist and it's all over."

"And you wouldn't suspect a woman," said Sloan slowly, "would you? I mean your defenses would be down, you would tend to trust her ..."

Dr. Dabbe gave a short, mirthless laugh. "My dear chap, I've no doubt you would, but then we do do very different jobs, don't we?"

The news had gone before Sloan to the Institute. There was that in the urgent way the porter hurried Sloan and Crosby to the Principal's room, in the curious stares of those students who just happened to be hanging about the entrance hall and in the manner of Marwin Ranby himself that told the policemen that they knew.

The Principal was visibly distressed. "I've just been trying to get in touch with the parents, Inspector, but I can't get a reply. It is Saturday lunchtime when not everyone's about—I was going away for the week-end myself as it happens—they may have done the same. They're farmers in the West Country, you know, Mr. and Mrs. Tewn, I mean, which is quite a way for them to come, I fear."

"A shocking business, sir."

"Terrible. The last few days have been quite bad enough, but this is a nightmare."

"Perhaps if you can tell us what happened, sir. ..."

"That's just it, Inspector. Nothing happened. I'd arranged to go over this morning to call on the Mother Superior to make the three of them apologize for their incursion into the Convent and for taking away the habit, which may have been old but which was doubtless of great significance to them. Celia—Miss Faine, you know—tells me that these garments are held to be very precious to the Sisters—they're handed down from one nun to another. I understand quite a number of them actually kiss each article of their habit before they put it on and so forth—and I felt it only right that these young men should say they were sorry in person. It's no use telling the young that these things don't matter, because they do."

Sloan jerked his head in agreement.

"I thought eleven-fifteen would do nicely. They only have two study periods on Saturday mornings and they finish at eleven and anyway that seemed to be as good a time as any for calling on the Mother Superior. I told them they were to present themselves here at five minutes past eleven to allow us time to walk over there …"

"One moment, sir. Whom did you tell to come then?"

Ranby frowned. "Bullen, Parker and Town, of course."

"Ah, I didn't mean quite that. To which one of the three did you give the message about the time?"

"Oh, I see. Bullen, it was. I told him to tell the other two. But only Bullen and Parker turned up. I must say, Inspector, I was more than a little cross at the time. And surprised. I wouldn't have said Town was the sort of man to back out of an interview like that, however unpleasant. It's horribly clear now, of course, why he didn't come."

"You just went off to the Convent without him?"

"Not at all. I sent Parker to his room to see if he was there and Bullen down to the Common Room. They both came back and said they couldn't find him and we then went off without him."

"How long did it take, sir?"

"Saying we were sorry? About five minutes. The Mother Superior was very gracious, thanked them for coming and more or less wrote it off as high spirits which—if I remember correctly—Bullen said was 'jolly decent of her in the circs'."

"The dead Sister—did she mention her?"

"Not at all."

"She tells me she had to keep you waiting."

"That's right. She was seeing another man. Largish, with gray hair. Town clothes, too. He came out of the Parlor as we went in."

Parker and Bullen were taking Town's death badly. They were sitting together at one end of the deserted Common Room. In the distance Sloan could hear luncheon being served, but it seemed Bullen and Parker were not hungry.

"I was sitting next to him at breakfast," said Bullen in a bemused way. "It doesn't seem possible, does it, that someone went and murdered him since?"

"When did you give him the message about going over to the Convent?"

Bullen stirred slowly. "I'd have to think. You know, I don't seem able to think straight, not now. Funny, isn't it?"

Sloan remembered the first sudden death that had come his way as a young constable. For years afterwards he had only had to shut his eyes for it all to come back to him. A road traffic accident that had been.

"You'll feel better in a day or so," he said automatically, "but you must try to think because we must know exactly what happened."

"He thought he told him before the first study period—at least that's what he told me earlier on." All the bounce had gone out of Parker, too. He was doing his utmost to be helpful. "He didn't see Tewn after that."

Sloan looked at Bullen. "That right?"

"Yes, Inspector. He should have been with us for the second study period—we're …" He stopped and corrected himself. "We were both in the second year, you see. But I didn't see him at all after we changed classrooms at ten o'clock. And neither did anyone else."

CHAPTER FOURTEEN

"I expect," observed Sloan to nobody in particular, "that it seemed a good idea to begin with, and the more you thought about it the better you liked it. After all, you'd got the fire all laid on—got to have a fire on Guy Fawkes' Night—you'd been gated too and there was the Convent practically next door, tempting Providence you might say almost." He paused. "And an old habit wasn't much compared with a bus shelter."

Bullen stirred. "We didn't think we were doing any harm. We didn't think it would end like this."

Parker retained more self-control. "But why should Town get killed? After all, we only swiped an old habit—there's no great crime in that, is there?"

"I think," said Sloan, "Town's crime was that he saw something."

"What?" asked Bullen dully.

"I don't know, but I'm hoping you two might. Listen—all three of you plan to get inside the Convent on Wednesday night to take an old habit. Of the three of you only Town actually goes inside. Of the three of you only Town gets killed."

"And that's not coincidence, you mean?" said the slow-thinking Bullen. He was paying more attention now, but he still looked like someone who has been hit hard.

"The police don't like coincidence," said Sloan. "Town went inside and Town was killed."

"Town *and* a nun," Parker reminded him. "We have to go and choose a night when a nun gets killed. There's a coincidence for you. I see what

113

you're getting at, though, Inspector. You mean that ..."

Sloan wasn't listening. A new and interesting thought had come to him. What had he just said himself? "The police don't like coincidences." There was one coincidence too many in what Parker had said.

"Listen both of you. I want you to go right back to the beginning and tell me where this idea about the habit came to you. And when."

"I don't know about where," said Bullen, "but I know when. Sunday, after supper. The Principal said we were to be gated from four o'clock on Guy Fawkes' Night because of what happened last year."

"Up till then what had you meant to do?"

Bullen looked a bit bashful. "Do you know Cherry Tree Cottage? It's on the corner by the Post Office."

"No."

"It's a funny little place with a rather awful woman in it. I don't know the word that describes it best but—"

"Twee," supplied Parker shortly.

"That's it. Well, she's got a garden full of those terrible things."

"What terrible things?" Bullen was hardly articulate.

"Gnomes," said Parker.

"And fairies," said Bullen, "and frogs and things. It's full of them. We thought—that is to say ..."

"This year's good cause?" suggested Sloan.

"That's it," said Bullen gratefully.

"I see. And when Mr. Ranby forestalled you?"

"Then we had to think of something else quickly."

"Whose idea was it to have a nun as a guy?"

Bullen shook his head. "I can't remember. Not mine."

"Nor mine," said Parker quickly. Too quickly.

"Can you remember," said Sloan sedulously, "whereabouts it was that this idea didn't come to you?"

"Oh, yes," said Bullen. "In The Bull. That's where we ..." He stopped.

"That's where you got on to Hobbett," Sloan finished for him.

Bullen flushed.

Sloan went on talking. "That's where you two and Tewn settled that Hobbett was to take the old habit from the garden room to the cellar and to leave the cellar door—the only one to which he had a key—open on Wednesday night. You were to creep in and take it away and you presumably showed your appreciation of Hobbett's—er—kindness in the usual manner. I'm not concerned just now with the rights and wrongs of all that.

What I want to know is: how many people knew you were going to be inside the Convent that night?"

Parker looked up intently. "I get you, Inspector. Quite a few, I should say, one way and another. Some of the men here for a start, the chap in charge of building the fire …"

"Anyone at The Bull?"

He frowned. "I dare say there might have been one or two. Hobbett's not the sort of man you'd want to sit down and talk to in the ordinary way, is he? He's quarrelsome and people mostly keep away from him. We sat with him in a corner for a while and led him round to it. It's pretty crowded in there at weekends—it's the only place in Cullingoak, and all the Institute men go there for a start. I reckon anyone seeing us could have put two and two together easily enough—we felt it was quite a good joke at the time."

"I think it's quite possible," said Sloan, "that someone else thought so too."

The day which had begun as routine continued that way, though in a different, more highly-geared groove. Superintendent Leeyes cancelled his regular Saturday afternoon fourball the better to superintend what had quickly become known as the Convent case.

Mr. Marwin Ranby cancelled his weekend away, spent the greater part of the afternoon on the telephone trying to get in touch with a remote farm in the West Country, and finally prevailed upon Miss Celia Faine to come round from the Dower House to the Institute for tea. That, at least, wasn't difficult.

For the Sisters it was perhaps a little easier. Saturday afternoon was for them a preparation for Sunday, a day without the significance of holiday or sport or relaxation. After Dr. Dabbe had gone and his next mournful job of work had been carried away in a plain black van, the Convent grille was closed and fifty women withdrew into their self-ordained silence. Not for them the endless unhappy speculation such as went round and round the Institute, nor the wild rumor piled upon fantasy that was tossed rapidly round the village. (Of its two institutions, Cullingoak was quite happy to exaggerate what went on at the Convent and to condemn out-of-hand the goings-on at the Institute.)

All in fact that did go on at the Convent was what anywhere else would have been termed a council of war. The Mother Prioress summoned those Sisters concerned in the finding of the dead William Town to

the Parlor. They filed in silently, distributing themselves in an orderly circle—
the neat Sister Ninian, the ebullient Sister Hilda, Sister Gertrude, Sister
Lucy, a young Sister who had been with Sister Lucy when Sloan arrived,
Sister Polycarp, the keeper of the gate who knew all comings and goings,
and three others who had happened upon the scene of the crime. Lacking
guidance about the correct religious behavior in the unusual circumstances
the three had stayed and moreover had failed lamentably to practice custody of the eyes. Now they wondered if having seen they should have
moved immediately away … truly it was a difficult path they had chosen
when they left the world.

The Mother Prioress began as she always did without preamble. "There
has been another murder. Not, as you know, a member of the Community,
but a student. He was killed in our grounds some time before recreation
this morning—at least that is the police view. The alternative is that he
was killed somewhere else and brought to the Convent grounds. Those of
you who have seen him would agree it is very unlikely. No, I fear our
connection with this particular student is closer than that. He is the one
who came into the Convent on Wednesday for the old habit which was
subsequently rescued by Inspector Sloan from the guy on the Institute
bonfire. Do I make myself clear?"

It was an unnecessary question. The Mother Prioress always made
herself clear.

"Therefore," she continued lucidly, "we still have a grave problem very
near at hand. Sister Anne was killed here in the Convent. This boy William
Tewn—God rest his soul—who was the one to enter the Convent on
Wednesday has also been killed. Until both crimes have been solved com-
pletely we are none of us in a position to know that no member of the
Community is involved."

She waited for this more oblique point to be appreciated.

"Moreover, we are bound by certain other considerations. Murder is
not normally the action of a normal human being, still less that of a religious. But it can be the abnormal action of an abnormal person. That is
the fact that we cannot overlook however much we might wish to."

The cheerful face of Sister Hilda clouded over as the significance of
this struck home.

"In the ordinary way," went on the Mother Prioress, "it would never be
necessary for me to ask you to tell me of anything untoward in the behavior of your Sisters, but we are not in the ordinary way. Far from it. We are
somewhere now outside our experience, and there can be no peace of

mind until the unhappy soul who has perpetrated these two crimes has been found and relieved of the terrible burden of their guilt."

It wasn't how Sloan would have put it, but it came to the same thing.

"You mean, Mother, one of us might have done it?" Sister Hilda looked quite astounded.

"I trust not, but temporary—or permanent—aberration is never impossible."

Sister Ninian nodded agreement. "Any one of us could have slipped out into the grounds before recreation and just stayed out and come in with the others afterwards. ..."

"Surely not!" exclaimed Sister Lucy.

Sister Polycarp looked down at her own strong hands. "They say he wasn't very big."

Sister Lucy shivered. "But who—which one of us could possibly have wanted ..."

"Have needed?"

"... have needed to do a terrible thing like that?"

"Two terrible things," put in the Mother Prioress quietly.

Sister Ninian frowned. Her hair, if she had had any hair, would have been gray by now, turned by the passing years, as her eyebrows had been, to a pale grayish blur above her blue eyes. "This means, Mother, doesn't it, that there is a connection between the two deaths?"

"A strong connection," said the Mother Prioress. "One so strong that the police feel they must interview every Sister today. They are particularly anxious that the details of the second crime of which you are already aware should not be communicated to the rest of the Community. I have undertaken that you will not discuss it either with them or with anyone else. I do not need to remind you that you are under obedience in this respect."

There was a series of assorted nods.

"The police," said the Mother Prioress, "have intimated to me that they consider it essential that these interviews are conducted by them with each Sister alone. It is not a procedure to which in the ordinary way I would have ever given my consent. As I have said before, we are no longer in the ordinary way. I have communicated with the Very Reverend Mother General at our Mother House and with Father MacAuley. Both are of the opinion that this is not an unreasonable request. And Inspector Sloan has sent to Calleford for a—er—lady policewoman."

"Luston?" barked Superintendent Leeyes. "What the devil do you want to go to Luston for?"

"To see a Miss Eileen Lome, sir."

"Are you going to tell me why, Sloan, or do I have to ask you?"

"She was a nun, sir, until about three weeks ago when she left the Convent of St. Anselm."

"Why?"

"I couldn't rightly say, sir. The Mother Prioress said she asked to be released from her vows and she was."

Leeyes's head went up like a bloodhound getting a scent. "Trouble in the camp?"

"Perhaps."

"We should have been told before."

"Yes, sir."

"Luston's not very far."

"No, sir. I thought I could go there while I wait for Sergeant Perkins to get over here from Calleford."

The superintendent gave a wolfish grin. "Sent for Pretty Polly, have you?"

"Yes, sir. I can't make headway in an interview with the Mother Prioress supervising and a couple of others sitting around for good measure. I want them on their own."

Leeyes nodded. "What about the Institute?"

"No joy there, sir. Town's fellow conspirators can't or won't help much. Can't—I think. Bullen can't remember anything Town said about the inside of the Convent that might give us any sort of lead. It might come to him, I suppose, though there's not much between his ears. Except bone. They're both trying to think hard of everything Town said or did since then."

"Cartwright?"

"Gone into Berebury for the afternoon. Left The Bull as soon as he'd had his lunch."

"Before you got there?"

"Yes, sir." Sloan wasn't going to start apologizing at this stage. "He says he'll be back, and he's left all his papers and clothes and so on. Besides, I've got a man at the London end checking up on Cartwright's Consolidated Carbons, and this business about their going public on Thursday. He wasn't all that pleased to be setting about it on a Saturday afternoon either."

"Duty first," said the superintendent virtuously. He looked at the clock. His erstwhile golfing cronies would be at the seventh tee about now. Superintendent Leeyes had lost two balls there last Saturday afternoon—driven them straight into the rough. "Cartwright will come back, I suppose? Because if not—"

"Our trouble has been surely that he's here in the first place," objected Sloan. "Practically underfoot, he's been. He's got motive, all right. But he's got brains too. Enough brains not to come knocking on the door out of the blue asking for Cousin Josephine if he dotted her on the head the night before."

"It's very nice for him that she's dead," said Leeyes. "Very nice. Now he can go ahead and turn his private firm into a nice little public company with heaven only knows what benefits to the principal shareholders."

"Death duty," said Sloan absently. "From her father's will, Sister Anne's share reverts to her uncle on her death without issue, which is fair enough. If they turn it into a public company while she's alive she can have a say in everything because she's got a fifty per cent stake in the capital. And you can't run a chemical company from a convent. If they leave it alone then she and uncle will each have to pay out a walloping proportion of the entire value of the firm in death duties sooner or later."

"This way?" asked Leeyes silkily.

"This way they go public on Thursday and transfer large blocks of shares round the family—Harold's children—grandchildren for all I know—some for the trusty members of the Board—that sort of thing."

"And I suppose you can also tell me why they didn't sell the whole boiling lot years ago?"

"Yes, sir. Then there wouldn't have been a job for our Harold Cartwright as Managing Director, and I fancy he enjoys being Managing Director of Cartwright's Consolidated Carbons. Besides, Sister Anne's consent would have been necessary but not, I fancy, forthcoming."

"Well then," snapped Leeyes, rounding on him, "why haven't you arrested Cartwright? You've got a case."

"A case for arresting him," conceded Sloan. "Not much of a case against him."

"Sloan."

"Sir?"

"You aren't hatching a case against one of those nuns, are you? I don't fancy having the whole Force excommunicated."

"I'm not hatching a case against anyone, sir. I don't think we can rule out anyone at all yet. The only apparent motive is Harold Cartwright's, and it's a bit too apparent for my liking. Of course, it may not be the only one. …"

"Hrrmph," trumpeted Leeyes. "There's still nothing to prove that the nuns *aren't* involved. One of them's dead inside their own Convent, killed by a weapon that was left around for another of them to touch—haven't found that yet, have we, Sloan?"

"No, sir."

"And then the student who goes inside goes and gets himself killed on eighteen inches of fuse wire—I suppose there's plenty of that in the Convent?"

"Plenty, sir. A whole reel by the fusebox by the door out of Hobbett's little lodge …"

"Hobbett … there's always Hobbett, of course. What about Hobbett? You haven't missed him, too?"

"Not exactly missed him, sir. He went off into Berebury at lunchtime with his wife like he does every Saturday lunchtime."

"Before they found Tewn?"

"He'd gone before we got there. I should say he knocks off sharpish."

"So you don't know for sure?"

"No, sir. But we've got every man in Berebury looking out for him."

"You've got a hope," said Superintendent Leeyes, "and on a Saturday afternoon, too."

CHAPTER FIFTEEN

Ironically enough it was Harold Cartwright who turned up first. At the Police Station. Crosby led him into Sloan's room.

"You've had another death," he said abruptly.

"I fear so."

"Where is this all going to end, Inspector?"

"I wish I knew, sir."

"First my cousin Josephine and now this student. It doesn't make sense."

"Murder doesn't always. Not to begin with."

"This boy—did my cousin know him?"

Usually it was Sloan who asked the questions, other people who answered them. Clearly Harold Cartwright, too, was in the habit of asking the questions that other people answered. Sloan let him go on that way. Questions revealed quite as much as answers; especially the ones that didn't get asked.

"William Tewn? No, sir, we have no reason to suppose that Sister Anne knew him. Have you?"

"Me, Inspector? I told you I haven't had sight nor sound of Josephine in twenty years."

"So you did, sir. I was forgetting."

Cartwright looked at him suspiciously. "And it's true."

"Yes, sir. We know that. Visitors and letters are both rationed in a convent."

"Like a prison," said Cartwright mordantly. "Poor Josephine."

Sloan pushed a blotter away. Not tonight, Josephine. Nor any night, Josephine. Poor Josephine.

"And yet," went on Cartwright, "Josephine and this young man Town have both been killed this week."

"That is so," acknowledged Sloan.

"Town saw something that gave him a lead on Josephine's murder?"

"That's the obvious conclusion, isn't it, sir? We're working on that now." So obvious that even the police couldn't miss it?

"So someone kills Town, too, to stop him talking?"

"Just so," said Sloan. It could even be that way.

"This is Saturday. How did—er—whoever did it—know that Town hadn't talked about what he saw?"

"There are at least three answers to that, sir, aren't there?" Sloan was at his most judicial. "One is that he didn't know if Town had talked or not, another is that Town saw something all right on Wednesday but that it didn't register as important until he heard that a nun had died that night. ..."

"And the third?"

"The third is that whoever killed Town might not have known until yesterday the name of the student who went inside the Convent. He might not have known who it was he had to kill, just as we didn't know ourselves until yesterday evening. Just as you didn't know who it was either, sir."

"But I did," Cartwright said unexpectedly.

"You did? Who told you?" Sloan snapped into life.

"He did himself. At least I take it it was the same lad."

"When?"

"On Thursday night at the fire. They were all standing round watching—like you do with a bonfire—waiting for the guy to catch alight. It was before you came along and did your brand-snatched-from-the-burning act."

"Well?"

"I was standing with a bunch of 'em when I realized they'd got a nun up top as a guy. I made some damn silly remark about that being a path not leading to Rome and how had they managed to get the full rig. One of them said he and another chap had done it and it had been dead easy."

"The vocabulary rings true," said Sloan, leaning forward. "Now what else did he say? Think very carefully, sir, this may be important."

Cartwright frowned. "Blessed if I can remember. No, wait a minute. There was something. The other chap with him made some sort of remark … 'Easy as stealing milk from blind babies.' That was it, and the first chap—the one who told me he'd got the habit …"

"Tewn."

"He laughed and said he reckoned it was all a matter of getting the milk warm enough—if you did that everything else was all right."

"Do you know what he meant?"

"No, Inspector, but the others all laughed at that. It sounded like some sort of Institute joke. Or even an agricultural one."

Sloan made a quick note. "Now, about the fire, sir. You did tell me how it was you came to be there, didn't you?"

"I did, Inspector," he said without rancor, "but I will tell you again if you wish."

Sloan inclined his head; and then regretted it. The eternal politeness of the nuns was quite infectious. He, a hardened Police Officer, would have to watch it.

"I was sitting in the bar of The Bull," said Cartwright, "on Thursday evening at something of a loose end. It is very unusual for me to have any free time, you understand. Also, I had only a few hours before been told by you of my cousin's premature death and I was not quite sure what was to be done about it. I meant to go out for a walk round the village to clear my thoughts a bit in any case, but when I heard some old man in a corner of the bar talking about a big bonfire at the Institute I thought I might walk that way."

"Substitute 'dirty' for 'old,' " said Sloan, "and you could be talking about a man I want to see."

"Hobbett was the name," said Cartwright. "I found that out afterwards. Contentious fellow. He was sitting there dropping hints about fun and games at the Institute. Apparently last year on Bonfire Night the students—"

"I know all about that," said Sloan wearily.

"This man was saying more-or-less that for the price of a drink he could tell a tale, and I decided to take my walk."

Sloan nodded. You could see why Cartwright was a captain of industry. He didn't waste words and he stuck to the point. He was giving just the right impression of anxious helpfulness, too, and so far had told Sloan just one thing that he didn't know already. Sloan eyed his visitor's figure. Business luncheons hadn't left too much of a mark there. He was only medium tall but strong enough to swing a weapon (somewhere between a paperweight and a cannonball) down on the head of an unsuspecting woman. Not everyone's cup of tea, but then not everyone could run one of the largest private companies in the land either. You couldn't begin to work out where scruple and resolution came in—perhaps not too much of one and plenty of the other for both. He didn't know. He was only a policeman.

"But it really comes down," Cartwright was saying, "to asking who could possibly have wanted to kill my cousin Josephine."

"Just you," said Sloan pleasantly.

There was no spluttering expostulation. "I didn't kill her," said Harold Cartwright.

"Perhaps not," said Sloan. "But it's saved you a lot of trouble, hasn't it?"

The man eyed him thoughtfully. "I'm not sure, yet. That's why I've come to see you. To ask for something."

"You don't want," said Sloan gently, "the chairman of Cartwright's Consolidated Carbons to be publicly connected with the late Sister Anne of the Convent of St. Anselm at Cullingoak who died in dubious circumstances on Wednesday—which is why you have stayed here in this village holding yourself ready for questioning rather than gone back to London where we should have had to come to see you."

"Inspector, should you ever leave the police and want a job, come to see me."

"Thank you, sir, but I feel I've earned my pension. And I'm going to enjoy it. This request for no publicity—I take it that you would like it to hold good until after one minute past ten on Thursday morning?"

Cartwright exhaled audibly. "Just until then, Inspector. It's very important."

"So," said Sloan, "is murder."

Bullen came to the telephone readily enough.

"Warm milk?" he echoed stupidly.

"Something about milk," said Sloan. "Think, man, think. What exactly did Tewn say about warm milk?"

"Nothing," said Bullen promptly.

Sloan sighed. "A witness has told me that while you were watching the guy burn, Tewn made some remark about warm milk. …"

"Oh, that," said Bullen. "I didn't know you meant that."

"I do mean that."

"I should have to think, Inspector."

Sloan waited as patiently as he could while Bullen's thought processes ground their way through his memory.

"There was this man there …"

"What man where?"

"Some town fellow, a stranger, who came to see the fire. He made some sort of crack about the nun's habit and our getting hold of it. I said it was dead easy."

"As easy as stealing milk from blind babies?"

"That's right, Inspector, and Tewn said it was all a matter of getting the milk warm enough."

"What did he mean?"

"He was being funny, Inspector. We'd been having a study lesson on feeding calves that afternoon. We'd all been having a bash—all the second year that is—when the Principal came in and said it was all a matter of getting the milk warm enough and then everything else would be all right."

"Oh, I see," said Sloan.

"Jolly clever of poor old Tewn, wasn't it? Made us all laugh at the time. All the second year anyway. Was there anything else, Inspector, that you wanted to know?"

"What? No, no thank you, Bullen. That was all."

Luston was the biggest town in Calleshire. Calleford had its Minister, its county administration, its history. Luston got on with the work.

Sloan and Crosby found Frederick Street in the decayed, once genteel, now shabby quarter of the town, bypassed alike by the glass self-service stores and the council's redevelopment schemes. They were there well before four o'clock, having fought their way through the crowded shopping center into the suburbs. Most of the inhabitants of Luston seemed to be out shopping—but not the occupant of 144 Frederick Street. The lace curtain twitched as the car drew up at the door, but for all that it seemed an age before the door was opened. A woman stood there, ineffectually dressed in clothes off the peg, her hair combed oddly straight.

"Good afternoon?" she said uncertainly.

"Miss Eileen Lome?" It couldn't be anyone else, thought Sloan, not with that hair.

She nodded.

"I wonder if you could spare us a moment or two? We want to talk to you about the Convent of St. Anselm."

Her face lit up spontaneously and then darkened. "You're not from the Press?"

"No, I'm Detective-Inspector Sloan of the Berebury C.I.D. and this is Constable Crosby, my assistant."

"That's different. Won't you come in?" She led the way through to the sitting room. "I don't want to talk to the Press. It wouldn't be right."

"We quite understand." Sloan was at his most soothing. "We shan't keep you long."

The sitting room was aggressively tidy. Miss Lome ushered them into easy chairs and chose a wooden one for herself.

"I can't quite get used to soft chairs yet," she said.

Sloan stirred uncomfortably in a chair he wouldn't have had inside his own home let alone sat in. "No, miss."

"Can I make you some tea?" suggested Miss Lome. "My sister's not back yet, but I think I know where everything is."

"No, thank you, miss. We'd like to talk to you instead."

She cocked her head a little to one side attentively. Sloan put her at forty-five, perhaps a trifle more. There was a youthful eagerness about her that made guessing difficult.

"When did you leave the Convent?"

"Twenty-four days ago."

"Why? I'm sorry—it's such a personal question, I know, but we have to …"

"I began to have doubts as to whether mine was a true vocation."

"How long were you there?"

"Twenty-five years."

"Twenty-five years?"

"Time has a different meaning there," she said tonelessly.

"Nevertheless," persisted Sloan, not unkindly, "it's quite a while, isn't it? One would have thought …"

"It's different," she said defensively, "for those who come in later. They seem more—well—sure, somehow. They know that all they want then is to be there, and they've proved it to themselves, and in any case they're older."

Sloan nodded. The word she was looking for was "mature." He did not supply it.

"But for the rest of us," she said, "who think we are sure at seventeen—you can't help but wonder, you know. And it grows and grows, the feeling that you aren't a true daughter of the Church." She shook her head sadly. "It is a terrible thing to lose your vocation."

Crosby's face was a study.

"I'm sure it is, miss," said Sloan hastily. And it was no use asking a policeman where to find one of them. They didn't deal in lost vocations. "So they let you out, miss?"

"It wasn't quite as simple as that, but that's what happened in the end." She brushed a hand across her straggly hair. She made it into a gauche, graceless gesture. "It's getting a bit less strange now. My sister's taken me in, you know. She's being very kind though she doesn't understand how very different everything is. Every single thing."

"Yes, miss, it must be."

The disaffection of the former Sister Bertha, now restored to her old name of Eileen Lome, seemed unlikely to have any bearing on the death of Sister Anne. In that the Mother Superior appeared to be quite right. Sloan sighed. It had seemed such a good lead. Apart from making quite sure…

"I don't know if you've had any news from the Convent lately," he said.

"You mean about Sister Anne? My sister showed me the newspaper this morning." She smiled wanly. "She thought it would interest me."

"You knew her well, of course?"

"Of course, Inspector. We had shared the same Community life for over twenty-five years."

"Tell me about her," urged Sloan gently.

Miss Lome needed no persuading. "She was professed about four years before me—the year I became a postulant, I think it was, though it's rather a long time ago for me to be sure. She had given up a very gay life in London, you know, to become a nun." Miss Lome glanced round the modest sitting room, economically furnished, plainly decorated. "Dances, parties, the London Season—that sort of thing. Her family had money, I think. …"

Sloan nodded.

"It used to worry Sister Anne a lot," volunteered Miss Lome.

"What did?"

"All that money."

Sloan read the look on Crosby's face as easily as if it had been the printed word. A lot of money wouldn't have worried him, it said. Just give him the chance and he'd prove it.

"In what way did it worry her?" asked Sloan.

"It was where it had all come from, Inspector, that was what she thought wrong. It was some sort of manufacturing process that was very valuable in making munitions in the First World War. But half the firm was to be hers one day, and then she intended to make restitution."

Sloan felt a momentary pang of sympathy for Cousin Harold.

"She always took an interest in foreign missions," continued Miss Lome. "She thought it was a way in which she could atone."

The look on Crosby's face, still easily readable, had changed to incredulity.

"She intended to sell out her interest in the firm?"

"That's right. As soon as it came to her."

"And this was common knowledge?"

Miss Lome gave a quick jerk of her head. "We knew it was something that worried her."

"All those years?"

"Time," said Miss Lome again, ruefully, "has a different meaning in a religious house."

She might have left the Convent but she had brought with her the training of a lifetime. When not speaking her eyes dropped downwards, and her hands lay folded in her lap. In gawky, unsuitable clothes, face and figure innocent of makeup or artifice, the mannerisms of the nun bordered on the grotesque.

"Nevertheless," said Sloan pedantically, "you must have been very surprised and shocked to read about the murder. …"

Another quick jerk of the head. "I've been trying so hard not to think about the past—until today. Now, I can't think about anything else except poor Sister Anne." She brightened with an effort. "But one mustn't dwell on the bad things, must one? There were some very happy times, too." She stared at him through a mist of tears and said wistfully, "When everything seemed quite perfect."

"Yes, miss, I'm sure there were. Tell me, have you been tempted to go back at all since you left?"

A curious color crept over her face, and Crosby looked quite startled. Miss Lome was actually blushing.

"Just to the gate, Inspector. Not inside. There's a part of the Convent you can see from the road if you know where to look. …"

"The newspaper photographer found it."

"That's right. I've been back as far as there—just to have a look, you understand. Silly and sentimental of me, I suppose."

"When?"

"Funnily enough, it was this morning."

CHAPTER SIXTEEN

"All right, all right," challenged Superintendent Leeyes. "You tell me of someone who wasn't at the Convent this morning for a change. The whole bang shooting match were there if you ask me—Hobbett, Cartwright, MacAuley, Ranby, Bullen, Parker, fifty nuns and now this woman. Anyone could have killed Tewn. Anyone. It's a wonder he wasn't trampled to death in the crowd."

"This woman says she just went as far as the gate, sir."

"Tewn didn't go much farther himself, did he? And look what happened to him."

"Yes, sir."

"And as for her saying she just went as far as the gate, how do you know that? How do we know she didn't go farther than the gate on Wednesday? Suppose she's the answer to it being an inside job or an outside one—a bit of both, in fact? What's to stop her coming in on Wednesday, slipping into the back of the Chapel for one of their eternal services and then waiting behind afterwards? You tell me the nuns don't know who comes into their Chapel from outside for services. Then all she has to do is to wait somewhere until just after supper. She knows where to find that old habit. And how to behave in it."

"Yes, sir."

"Then, after supper she waits in that corridor with a weapon that you've proved to me must have come from the Convent though you can't find it."

"No, sir."

"Then she kills Sister Anne, hears someone coming and pushes her into the broom cupboard. Probably goes inside with her. And at half past eight she creeps out for some service or other."

"Vespers."

"To stop the hue and cry being raised until the morning. She goes in last, knowing the others are too damn ladylike to look up, pretends she's got a cold and keeps her face buried in a handkerchief. Probably comes out last, too, then while the others go up to bed she sidles down the corridor and hides somewhere until it's all quiet."

"The necessarium?" offered Sloan.

"The what?"

"The smallest room, sir."

The superintendent turned a dull shade of purple. "Very probably, Sloan, very probably. I was forgetting," he added savagely, "that they aren't fairies. Then when all the others are tucked up in their nice warm cells, she comes out of there and pops into the broom cupboard, heaves Sister Anne's body down the cellar steps, and lets herself out through the cellar door and legs it back to Luston."

Sloan studied the ceiling. "Leaving the habit in the cellar for Tewn, who comes along ten minutes later and takes it away?"

Leeyes glared.

"Or alternatively," went on Sloan, switching his gaze to the floor, "she just happens to discard the habit there and Tewn just happens to come along and pick it up?"

"Tewn came there by arrangement, didn't he?" Leeyes shifted his ground with subtlety.

"With Hobbett, sir. He promised to have the habit there for the students and to leave the outside cellar door open."

"Someone knew about that little conspiracy, Sloan."

"Yes, sir, unless …"

"Unless what?"

"It was a totally inside job. Then it wouldn't have mattered what happened to the outside cellar door or the habit."

"Who would have been lying?"

"Sister Damien."

Leeyes shrugged. "I don't like coincidence. Never have done."

"Neither do I, sir, but you must allow for it happening."

The superintendent gave an indeterminate growl. "What next?"

"Back to the Convent with Sergeant Perkins, sir."

"Have they brought Hobbett in yet?"

"Not yet, sir."

"There's always the chance, I suppose," said Leeyes hopefully, "that he'll stand on one of them's toe. …" The other three golfers would be coming up the eighteenth fairway by now—without him. "Sloan …"

"Sir?"

"This woman, Eileen Lome—why did she leave the Convent?"

"She lost her vocation," said Sloan, shutting the door behind him very gently indeed.

Sergeant Perkins was in his room when he got back.

He nodded briskly. "What do you know about Convents, Sergeant?"

"That they're not allowed to have mirrors there," she said. She was a good-looking girl herself.

"Poor things," said Sloan unsympathetically. "Now, about the case …"

She flung a smile at his assistant. "Constable Crosby has been putting me in the picture, Inspector."

Sloan grunted. "It's not a pretty one. Two murders in four days. I don't know about your end of the county, but out of the ordinary run for us."

"And us, sir. Just husband and wife stuff as a rule."

Sloan picked up the sheets of paper the Mother Superior had sent him that morning. "They've given us a list of every nun in the place, her—er—given name and her religious one, and what she said she was doing after supper on Wednesday. Now I suppose we shall need to know what they said they were doing this morning."

"Never mind, sir, it's nearer than Wednesday. They're not as likely to have forgotten."

"There is that," admitted Sloan. He'd obviously got an optimist on his hands, which made a change from the superintendent.

"How many are there of them, sir?"

"Just over fifty." That should deaden anyone's enthusiasm for interviewing. "And all falling over themselves backwards not to be too observant, inquisitive or whatever else you like to call it."

She nodded.

"And," he added for good measure, "they don't seem to think it's right to have normal human feelings about people. Have you ever tried interviewing people without normal human feelings, Sergeant?"

"Often, Inspector. I get most of the teenage work in Calleford."

He did not laugh. Nobody in the Calleshire Constabulary ever laughed at the word "teenager."

He turned to Crosby. "Any luck with that list?"

"Yes, sir. There are four nuns who came into the Order late like Miss Lome said. Sister Margaret, Sister Lucy, Sister Agatha and Sister Philomena. Judging by all the other dates and ages the rest came in straight from school."

"Poor things," said Sergeant Perkins impulsively.

"And the other four?"

"Late twenties—one, early thirties—two, early forties—one."

"Which one was that?"

"Sister Agatha. She came here from"—he flipped the sheets over—"the Burrapurindi Mission Hospital."

"It's a republic now," said Sloan briefly. "And the other late entries?"

"Sister Philomena and Sister Margaret seem to have been schoolteachers first."

"The blackboard jungle."

"And Sister Lucy"—he turned the pages back—"there's no occupation down for her—just that she came from West Laming House, West Laming. It's not the best address though, sir."

"No?"

"No, sir. One of them comes from a castle. Fancy leaving a castle to go and live in a convent."

"Probably the only one who didn't notice the cold. Which one was that?"

"Sister Radigund."

Sloan nodded. "You might think Sister Agatha was the one to be in charge of the sick if she had been a nurse, but I suppose that would be too simple for them."

"There's a Lady, too, sir."

"They're all ladies, Crosby, that's their trouble."

"No, sir. I mean a real one. It says so here. Lady Millicent."

"And what's she now?"

"Mother Mary St. Bridget."

Sergeant Perkins leaned forward. "Some are Mothers, are they then, Inspector?"

"A courtesy title, Sergeant, I assure you. For long service, I believe."

Crosby made a noise that could have been a hiccup.

Sloan favored him with a cold stare. "Was there anything else, Crosby?"

"Just the Mother Superior, sir."

"What about her?"

"Her name was Smith, sir. Mary Smith of Potter's Bar."

The three of them stood on the Convent doorstep and rang the bell. It was quite dark now. They could hear the bell echoing through the house, and then the slow footsteps of Sister Polycarp walking towards them.

Sergeant Perkins shivered. "The only other thing I know about nuns is that they used to be walled up alive if they did anything wrong."

Sloan was not interested. As a police officer he was concerned with crime, not punishment.

"There was the nun who was murdered in Thirteen Fifty-One," proffered Crosby unexpectedly. "By a crazy younger son."

"And which was she?" demanded Sloan.

In the reflected light of the outer hall Crosby could be seen to be going a bit red. He gulped and chanted:

"An extremely rowdy nun
Who resented it.
And people who come to call
Meet her in the hall.

"The Police Concert," he stammered hastily. "We sang it—four of us—it's Noël Coward's."

Sister Polycarp pulled the bolts of the door back. "Sorry to keep you. I was in the kitchen."

"That's all right," said Sloan. "Constable Crosby here has been entertaining us with a refrain of Mr. Noël Coward's."

"Coward?" Polycarp sniffed. "Can't say I've heard the name. Ought I to have done?"

Sloan looked at her respectfully. "Oh, Sister, you don't know what you gave up when you left the world."

"Oh, yes, I do, young man. Believe you me I do."

The former Mary Smith of Potter's Bar, now Mother Superior of the Convent of St. Anselm, was in the Parlor to greet them.

Sloan introduced Sergeant Perkins. "I'm very sorry about this further intrusion, marm, but my superintendent insists …"

"But our Bishop agrees, Inspector, so pray do not worry on that score. We appreciate your difficulties."

An hour later he wondered if she did.

It was slow, painstaking work, seeing nun after nun, each with eyes demurely cast down, voices at low, unobtrusive pitch, each having to be asked specifically each question.

"What did you do immediately after supper on Wednesday evening, Sister?"

"The washing up, Inspector."

"The vegetables for the next day, Inspector."

"Prepared the Chapel, Inspector."

"Swept the refectory, Inspector."

"Some lettering on prayer cards, Inspector."

"A little crochet, Inspector."

"There was a letter I was permitted to write, Inspector."

"Studied a book on the life of our Founder, Inspector."

And to each one: "When did you last see Sister Anne?"

As one woman they replied: "At supper, Inspector."

Someone had been in her stall at Vespers, they knew that now, but they had no suggestions to make. None had seen anything untoward then or at any other time. Or if they had they weren't telling Sloan and that good-looking young woman he had with him.

It was not noticeably different when he asked about that morning.

The same pattern of cleaning, cooking, praying emerged.

"Admin stuff," he observed to Sergeant Perkins in between nuns.

"They don't look unhappy," she said.

"I don't think they are. Once you've got used to it, I'm sure it's a great life."

She grinned. "Not for me, sir."

"No," said Sloan. "I didn't think it would be. Next please, Crosby."

There were faces he was beginning to know now. Characteristics were identifying themselves to him in spite of the strenuous efforts of their owners to suppress them.

Sister Hilda, whose lively, dancing eyes and harmonious voice belied her somber habit. She had seen nothing on Wednesday or Saturday.

"But that's not surprising, Inspector, is it? That corridor is pretty dim in daylight, let alone in the evening. And we don't exactly go in for bright lights here, do we? As for this morning—once you're out of range of the windows practically anything can happen."

"Could anyone leave the house unobserved?"

"Probably not, but," she said frankly, "anyone could go out into the grounds without anyone else asking why. It wouldn't be anything to do with them, you see, so they wouldn't notice properly if you know what I meant."

Then there was the thin-lipped Sister Damien, who unbent not one fraction without the restraining presence of the Mother Superior.

"Had I seen anything suspicious I would have told Mother immediately," she said.

"And this morning?"

"I was dusting the Library. I saw and heard nothing out of the ordinary."

"You know Miss Eileen Lome, of course?"

She shook her head. "The name means nothing to me, Inspector."

"Sister Bertha that was. …"

"Ah, yes." Her narrow features assumed a curious expression compounded of regret and disapproval. "The former Sister Bertha."

"Have you seen her since she left?"

"None of us have seen her, Inspector, since she renounced her vows. It would not have been proper."

And, nearly the last, Sister Lucy.

She came in and sat down, hands folded serenely in her lap, waiting expectantly for Sloan to speak.

"It's a little strange, Sister, interviewing you in your own Parlor, but—er—needs must. This is Sergeant Perkins who has come over from Calleford."

Two women in two very different uniforms regarded each other across the room. It did something for each, decided Sloan, but then uniforms usually did.

"You've got your keys back, Sister, I see."

She patted the huge bunch which hung from her girdle. "Yes, indeed, Inspector, my badge of office. I was lost without them."

"Sister, this dead boy, William Tewn, did you know him?"

"No, Inspector. I had never heard of him until this morning."

"Nor seen him before?"

She shook her head. "Never. Nor the two other boys who came over with Mr. Ranby. The students can be seen from the Convent grounds if they are working on their own land, but they're not usually near enough to identify and I'm sure no Sister would ever …"

"We have to ask any number of questions in our job," he said placatingly. "And they may seem irrelevant." But they weren't, he thought to himself. She had been pale and shaking when she met him at the Convent door this morning after the second murder. He had seen that with his own two eyes, which made it cold, hard evidence.

"Sister, you came later than most to the Convent …"

She bowed her head. "That is so. I've been professed for only ten years now."

It was quite comical to see Woman-Sergeant Perkins doing a quick calculation of Sister Lucy's age on the material available to her.

"Happy years?" queried Sloan.

"Everything was very strange at first, Inspector, but it gradually becomes a very rewarding way of life."

"Most of your—er—colleagues came here straight from school—it is permitted then to enter later?"

She nodded. "It is permitted, Inspector. It does not happen very often. I had not intended to become a nun when I left school, you see, but my aunt—I was brought up by an aunt—she was able to get dispensation from the Very Reverend Mother General."

"I see," said Sloan. "Thank you, Sister."

He didn't see, but Sergeant Perkins did.

"What's a good-looking woman like that doing in a Convent?" she asked shrewdly, when Sister Lucy had retired. "There's waste for you. Put her into a decent frock and she'll still stop the traffic. I'll bet she's got good legs, too. ..."

"We shall never know," said Sloan. "Shall we?"

"Of course," went on Sergeant Perkins, "all that shy stuff that they play at—eyebrow fluttering, not looking at you and that sort of thing—that's all very fetching anyway, but she's a real good-looker, isn't she?"

"It's double murder we're investigating," said Sloan dryly. "Not abduction. And it wasn't the good-looking one that bought it either. It was the one with the fifty per cent holding in Cartwright's Consolidated Chemicals."

"And she was plain?"

"Not as bad as some we've seen this afternoon," said Sloan fairly, "but plain enough."

Sergeant Perkins sighed. "So it wasn't her Sir Galahad at Vespers, disguised as a nun and come to rescue her?"

"If it was anyone at all," said Sloan, "it was the murderer."

"Like the joke says?"

"What joke?"

Sergeant Perkins opened her eyes wide. "Haven't you heard it, sir?"

"Not yet," said Sloan grimly, "but I'm going to. Now," he looked from one to the other, "Crosby, have you heard it?"

"Yes, sir. Often." He coughed bashfully. "They sing it every time I go into the canteen."

"Do they indeed? Suppose you sing it to me now. ..."

"Not sing it, sir. I can't sing."

"I want to hear it, Crosby, and fast."

Crosby cleared his throat and managed a sort of chant:

"You may kiss a nun once,
You may kiss a nun twice,
But you mustn't get into the habit."

CHAPTER SEVENTEEN

"That you, Sloan?"

Sloan held the Convent telephone receiver at a distance suitable for the superintendent's bellow.

"Leeyes here," said the voice unnecessarily.

"'Evening, sir."

"Just to let you know," trumpeted the superintendent, "that the rest of the Force haven't been idle while you've been sitting around in that Parlor with Sergeant Perkins."

"And fifty nuns, sir."

Leeyes chose not to hear this. "We've got Hobbett for you."

"Good," said Sloan warmly. "I want a few words with him."

"They picked him up in The Dog and Duck just after opening time."

"Keep him, sir, I'll be back."

"I wasn't proposing to let him go, Sloan, though he's invoking everyone you've ever heard of. And then some. They tell me he'd hardly had time to sink his first pint and he's very cross."

"That suits us nicely, sir. Can you leave him to cool off while I go on from here to the Institute? There's something I want to ask them there."

"I don't mind, Sloan, though I dare say the Station Sergeant might. However, you can make your own peace with him later. Talking of Sergeants, Sloan …"

"Sir …?"

"Sergeant Gelden's turned up at last. With that bigamist. Silly fool."

It was only fairly safe to assume he meant the bigamist.

"Do you want him back instead of Crosby?"

Sloan sighed. "No, sir. Not at this stage. I'll keep Crosby now I've got him, but if you can spare Gelden I'd very much like him to go to West Laming for me."

"Tonight?" They would have finished the nineteenth hole too before the superintendent got to the golf club. "Funny place to send a man on a Saturday night."

"Yes, sir." Sloan turned through the pages of his notebook, peering at his own handwriting. The electric light bulbs in this corridor couldn't be a watt over twenty-five. "I want him to find out all he can about a Miss Felicity Ferling, who left there about ten years ago."

"I suppose you know what you're doing, Sloan."

"Yes, sir." Someone had once said, "Never apologize, never explain." Someone with more self-confidence than he had. Disraeli, was it? "And tell him," added Sloan boldly, "to ring me from there. Not to wait until he gets back."

"He won't get back, not tonight anyway. It must be the best part of ninety miles away."

"Yes, sir, but if he starts now I should hear from him before ten."

The superintendent came in on another tack. "Getting anywhere with all those women?"

"I'm not sure, sir," parried Sloan. "They're a strange crew. Not like ordinary witnesses at all. They don't wonder about anything because they don't think it's right."

"Theirs not to reason why …" Leeyes didn't seem to see where the rest of that quotation was going to lead him. "Theirs but to do … and … er … die."

"Just so, sir," said Sloan.

Sergeant Perkins went with them to the Institute.

"I may need you," said Sloan. "I expect Ranby's fiancée will be there. She's got good legs and you can at least see 'em."

"No uniform?"

"I wouldn't say that. Classic wool twin set, single string of pearls, quiet tweed skirt …"

"One of those," said Sergeant Perkins feelingly.

"Nice girl all the same, I should say. She won't have abandoned Ranby at a time like this."

They found not only Celia Faine with Ranby in the Principal's room but Father MacAuley too.

"A sad, sad business," said the priest.

"Terrible," endorsed Ranby. "A young life like that just cut off. It doesn't make sense. Do you—may one ask—are you making any headway, Inspector?"

"In some ways," said Sloan ambiguously.

"His people will be here by midday tomorrow. Not that that's any help. We know who he is." The Principal looked older now.

"We don't know very much about him though," commented Sloan mildly.

"I can't say that we do either. One tends to know best those who come up against authority—sad but true—and Tewn wasn't one of those. He seemed a likeable lad; not an outstanding student, mark you, but a trier."

"He'd remembered one of the things you'd taught him," said Sloan.

Ranby twisted his lips wryly. "I'm glad to hear it. What was that?"

"Something about feeding the calves. All a matter of getting the milk warm enough."

The Principal's face stiffened. "Getting the milk warm enough?"

"That's right, sir. When you feed calves by hand, you taught them—on Thursday afternoon, was it?—that getting the calves to take the milk was all a matter of getting the milk warm enough."

"So I did," said Ranby warily, "but what's it got to do with Tewn's death?"

"I couldn't say," murmured Sloan equivocally. "I couldn't say at all. Now, sir, would you say this lad had any enemies?"

"Just the one," said Ranby dryly.

"What? Oh, yes, sir, I see what you mean. Very funny." Sloan sounded quite unamused.

"Poor lad," said Celia Faine. "At least he couldn't have known very much about it. Strangling's very quick, isn't it?"

"So I'm told, miss." He looked at her. "Sister Anne wouldn't have known all that much either, come to that. Just the one heavy blow."

The girl shivered. "It doesn't seen possible. Cullingoak's always been such a peaceful, happy village. And now ..." She made a gesture of helplessness. "Two innocent, harmless people are killed."

"Innocent," said Sloan sharply, "but not harmless. That's the trouble, isn't it?"

Father MacAuley nodded. "The boy was harmless until he got inside the Convent. Sister Anne—we may have thought she was harmless but someone wanted her dead. It wasn't an accident. It couldn't have been."

"Murder," said Sloan tersely. "Well planned and carried out." There was a small silence. "However, no doubt we shall find out in due course the person responsible and thence the murderer of this lad Tewn."

The priest nodded. "In due course, I'm sure you will. I've just left the Convent—they're not altogether happy about being left alone to-night without any male protector but they tell me you can't spare a man."

Sloan shook his head. "Sorry. Not on a Saturday evening. Any chance of your going back there, Father, for a while?"

"Me? Certainly, Inspector. I quite understand how they feel. Their experiences of the past four days are enough to make anyone feel apprehensive."

Ranby nodded. "I don't blame them either. I'll come across with you, Father, and see if we can't arrange something for tonight. What about their gardener fellow?"

"Hobbett? No," said Sloan regretfully. "You can't have him. We're keeping him at the station this evening for questioning. I shouldn't care to have the responsibility of leaving him as protector."

"Ranby and I will go across when they've had supper and Vespers then," said the priest, "and fix things so that they feel safer."

"So that they are safer," said the Principal.

"Thank you." Sloan rose to go. "There was just one thing I wanted to ask Miss Faine. …"

Celia Faine lifted her eyebrows enquiringly.

"You know the house better than anyone, miss?"

"Perhaps I do," she agreed. "I was a child there and children do explore."

"Tell me—it's an old house, I know—is there any place there that someone could hide? A priest's hole or anything like that?"

She smiled. "Not that I know of, Inspector. Nothing so romantic. Or exciting." She frowned. "It's large, I know, as houses go, but straightforward—the hall, the Chapel, the dining room—that's the refectory now, of course—one or two smaller rooms—the drawing-room was upstairs. I expect it's a dormitory now, and then the Long Gallery. I can't think what they'll have used that for. Nothing else. No mysteries." She smiled again. "The only thing I ever discovered as a child was the newel post at the bottom of the great staircase. My cousin and I were playing one day and we found the orb at the top lifted out. It's on a sort of stalk and it slides on and out quite easily. We used to play with that a lot."

"Round and smooth and heavy and staring you in the face," snapped Superintendent Leeyes. "Well, is there blood on it?"

"Dr. Dabbe's examining it now," said Sloan. "But it's been cleaned three times since Wednesday night, and when these nuns say clean they mean clean."

"Did that Sister with the blood on her hand ..."

"Peter."

"Did she touch it that morning?"

"She thinks she did. She won't swear to it, but she thinks she sometimes touches it."

"She thinks she sometimes touches it," mimicked the superintendent. "What a crowd! And did she sometimes touch it on Thursday morning?"

"She can't remember for certain. She might have done."

"When was it cleaned?"

"First thing after breakfast. Before Terce and Sext."

"What are ...?"

"Their Office, sir."

"Before they'd realized it was blood on that book?"

"The Gradual? Yes, sir. They didn't examine the book until afterwards. The staircase, landings and hall are always cleaned immediately after breakfast each day."

Leeyes drummed his fingers on the desk. "So it could still be anyone, Sloan."

"Anyone, sir, who knew that part of the newel post came out and would constitute a nice heavy weapon, ideal for murder."

Hobbett was easy meat really.

"You can't keep me here, Inspector. I haven't done nothing wrong and I can prove it. I wasn't running away neither. I allus come into Berebury Sat'day afternoons."

"What you did wrong, Hobbett, was agreeing to let those young gentlemen into the Convent. I know an old habit isn't worth much, but look at the trouble you've caused. And now you're involved in a double murder case whether you like it or not, aren't you?"

"I didn't 'ave nothing to do with no murder. I just fergot to lock up

Wednesday night, that's all. Clean went out of my mind."

"You arranged—for a small consideration," said Sloan in a steely voice, "to leave the old habit in your wood store in the cellar and to forget to lock up. And three students named Parker, Bullen and Tewn were to creep in and collect it. Tewn did the creeping and Tewn's dead."

"It weren't nothing to do with me," protested Hobbett. "I only did like you said. Moving an old piece of cloth from one place to another and forgetting to lock up—that's not a crime, is it? What's that got to do with murder?"

"Everything," said Sloan sadly. "It provided the opportunity."

The telephone was ringing as Sloan got back to his room.

Crosby handed over the receiver. "For you, sir. London."

"Inspector Sloan? Good. About our friends the Cartwrights and their Consolidated Chemicals. ..."

"Yes?"

"Something I think will interest you, Inspector."

"Yes?"

"Harold—the principal subject of our enquiry—highly respected, highly respectable business man. Hard but straight."

"Well?"

"His father—Joe—not such a good business man but quite a fellow with the chemicals in his day. Past it now, of course."

"Of course. He must be about eighty-five."

"That's just it. He is. And he had a stroke on Tuesday night. He's still alive but not expected to recover."

Sloan whistled. "So that's what upset the applecart!"

"At a guess—yes."

"Thank you," said Sloan. "Thank you very much."

"I'm glad it was useful information," said the voice plaintively, "because I should have been at Twickenham this afternoon."

Sloan pushed the telephone away from him.

"So, Crosby, if Sister Anne died before Uncle Joe all was well. If she consented to the firm going public all was not well but better than it might have been. If she neither died nor consented, Cousin Harold inherited his father's half minus death duties leaving Sister Anne with her half intact and a strong leaning to the Mission field and making restitution."

"Tricky," said Crosby.

"Tricky? Cousin Harold must have been in a cold sweat in case his father died before he got to Cullingoak and Sister Anne."

"Sir, what about that awful old woman we saw in London, Sister Anne's mother—doesn't she come into this?"

Sloan shook his head. "No. She's only got a life interest that reverts to either her daughter, brother-in-law or nephew according to the order in which they survive. We can leave her out of this. Give me that telephone back, will you? I'm going to ask Cousin Harold to go up to the Convent."

"Tonight?"

"Tonight, Crosby. After the good Sisters have had supper and Vespers."

Crosby started to thumb through the telephone directory.

"Crosby, where's Sergeant Perkins?"

"In the canteen, sir."

"Get them to save me something, and then tell her I want to see her. I'm going back to see the superintendent when I've spoken to Cousin Harold."

"It was blood then, Sloan."

"Yes, sir. Dr. Dabbe's just sent along his report. Minute traces, dried now and mixed with polish, but indubitably blood."

"Group?"

"The same as Sister Anne's, the same as on the Gradual."

"And as a possible weapon?"

"Ideal." Sloan tapped the pathologist's report. "He won't swear to it being the exact one …"

"Of course not," said Leeyes sarcastically. "They never will."

"But it fits in every particular."

"Good enough for the jury, but not the lawyers?"

"Yes, sir."

"And what do you propose to do now?"

Sloan told him.

CHAPTER EIGHTEEN

Neither the Mother Superior nor Sister Lucy were present at Vespers that Saturday evening. If any member of the Community so far forgot herself as to notice the fact, they took good care not to look a second time at the two empty stalls. The welfare of the Convent of St. Anselm sometimes necessitated their presence in the Parlor with visitors. So it was this evening.

There were three of them, and a grumbling Sister Polycarp had let them in and taken them to the Parlor. The Convent of St. Anselm did not usually have visitors at the late hour of eight- thirty in the evening and she resented the interruption of her routine. She would have resented still further—had she known about it—two other visitors who had come privily to another door a little earlier. They had tapped quietly on the garden room door that Sister Polycarp had so carefully locked and bolted only an hour before that. But it was mysteriously opened for them and they stepped inside, a man and a woman, locking it as carefully behind them as Sister Polycarp had done so that should she chance to check again there was nothing to show that it had been opened and closed again in the meantime.

The Mother Superior greeted those who had come by the front door, keeping Sister Polycarp by her side.

"Father, how kind of you to come back, and Mr. Ranby too."

"We don't like to think of you alone here all night with a murderer at large."

She bowed. "It is indeed difficult to sleep with that thought. We have been more than a little perplexed." She lowered her voice, "You see we cannot exclude the possibility that the—er—perpetrator of these outrages is within our own house."

Both men nodded.

"Especially," went on the Mother Superior, "now that the police have discovered the murder weapon was here all the time."

"They have?" said Ranby.

"The orb on the top of the newel post. Inspector Sloan has taken it away."

"Now, about tonight …" said the priest.

"Mr. Cartwright has come up from the village, too," said the Mother Superior. "He is just looking through the cellars for us now. We felt a little uneasy about the cellars."

"Yes, indeed," said Father MacAuley soothingly. "I think it would be as well if Cartwright, Ranby and I worked out some scheme for patrolling the building, cellars and all."

"We had already decided to do that ourselves," said the Mother Superior, "but if you would be so kind as to augment our—rather feminine efforts it would be a great kindness."

"An hour each on," suggested Ranby, "and two off. That is if Cartwright agrees?"

"Right," said MacAuley.

"With one Sister …"

"With two Sisters," said the Mother Superior firmly.

"With two Sisters in the gallery at the top of the stairs."

"Thank you, gentlemen. That should keep us safe through the night. I will detail the Sisters immediately. They are quite used to night vigils, you know. In Lent we keep them between the Offices of Compline and Lauds."

Sergeant Gelden rang Sloan at Berebury Police Station at a quarter to ten.

"That you, Inspector? About a Miss Felicity Ferling of West Laming House."

"I'm listening, Sergeant."

"It's like this, sir. …"

Sloan listened and he wrote, and he thanked Sergeant Gelden. Then he drove out to Cullingoak. He parked his car at The Bull and walked to the Convent from there, timing the walk. Then he, too, went round to the garden door and tapped very quietly. He was admitted by no less a personage than the Mother Superior herself.

She produced a list for him. "From ten to eleven, Father MacAuley and Sisters Ninian and Fidelia; from eleven to twelve Mr. Cartwright and Sisters Damien and Perpetua, and from twelve to one Mr. Ranby and Sisters Lucy and Gertrude."

"And so on through the night?"

"Yes, Inspector, unless anything untoward happens. Sister Cellarer has sent a supply of hot coffee and sandwiches to the Parlor for those not actually watching."

"Any difficulties?"

"None. All three gentlemen were quite agreeable to my suggestions."

"Let's hope they've swallowed everything. And the rest of the Community?"

"Gone to bed, Inspector, as usual."

"Good. And the arrangements for changing over the watch so to speak?"

"The retiring Sisters will knock on their successors' doors ten minutes before the hour."

"Excellent. Is Sister Lucy in bed?"

"Sister Lucy has perforce been in bed for some time now, Inspector." He gave her a quick smile. "We're nearly there, marm."

"Pray God that you are," she said soberly.

Sloan made himself as comfortable as he could in the flower room and settled down to wait. And to wonder.

If he opened the door the minutest fraction he could see the hall and its sentinel. First it was Father MacAuley who paced up and down the hall and then did a methodical round of doors and windows. Sloan had to retreat behind a curtain for that. And then Harold Cartwright, noisier than the priest, conscientiously poking about along the corridor and talking quietly up the stairs to Sister Damien and Sister Perpetua.

He heard them at about quarter past twelve and again at a quarter to one.

"Everything all right up there with you?"

"Yes, thank you, Mr. Cartwright. It's all quiet, thank God." Sister Damien's thin whisper came floating down the stairs in reply. "We're just going along to wake the others. We'll see you at two o'clock again."

"Right you are."

Sloan heard him do one last quick round and then nip back towards the Parlor. Then the Parlor door opened and Ranby came out. He came straight to the garden room, and Sloan was hard put to it to get behind his curtain in time. Ranby pulled back the bolts and left the door slightly ajar and then went back to the hall.

Sloan came out from behind his curtain and held the door open. Ranby was standing at the foot of the stairs, calling softly upwards.

"Are you there, Sister Lucy?"

Sister Gertrude came to the balustrade and leaned over. "We're both here, Mr. Ranby. Is there something wrong?"

"No. I just wanted a word with Sister Lucy about Tewn. It's something she said earlier this morning. It's just occurred to me it might be important."

Sister Gertrude withdrew and Sister Lucy appeared in her stead on the landing and began walking slowly down the polished treads, her head bent well down, her massive bunch of keys swinging from her girdle.

Ranby retreated a little as she descended, backing away from the small well of light in the hall, away from the gaze of Sister Gertrude. He came, as Sloan thought he would, towards the dark corridor where Sister Anne had died, the corridor where Sloan stood waiting and watching.

"Felicity," Ranby whispered urgently to her, "come this way. I must talk to you."

The nun turned obediently in his direction and walked exactly where he said.

"This way," he urged. "So that the others don't hear us."

She was almost level with him now, his eyes watching her every movement, not seeing at all the dim shadowy figure that was following her down the stairs, pressed against the furthest wall.

As she drew abreast of him he put up an arm as if to embrace her. It quickly changed to a savage grasp, his other hand coming up in front of her neck searching for soft, vulnerable cartilage and vital windpipe.

The eager questing fingers were destined to be disappointed in their prey.

The nun did a quick shrug and twist and Ranby let out a yelp of pain. The arm fell back, but he came in with the other. That did him no good at all. The nun caught it and flung herself forward against it. Ranby fell heavily, her weight on top of him.

And then Sloan was there and the dark shadow on the wall was translated into Detective-Constable Crosby with handcuffs at the ready. Along the corridor the Parlor door opened and Father MacAuley and Harold Cartwright came hurrying out.

The nun clambered off Ranby, hitching up her habit in an un-nunlike way. "These blasted skirts," she said, "certainly hamper a girl." She struggled out of the headdress and shook her hair loose. "But this is worse. Fancy having to live in one of these."

"That's not Sister Lucy," gasped Ranby.

"No," agreed Sloan. "That's Police-Sergeant Perkins in Sister Lucy's habit."

CHAPTER NINETEEN

"I didn't think it would come off a second time," said Sloan modestly.

The superintendent grunted. He didn't usually reckon to come in to the station on a Sunday morning, but then his Criminal Investigation Department didn't arrest a double murderer every day of the week. Sloan, Perkins, Gelden and Crosby were all present—and looking regrettably pleased with themselves.

"No snags at all?" asked Leeyes.

"Worked like a charm," said Sloan cheerfully. "He was quite taken in by Sergeant Perkins. So was I, sir. Anyone would have been."

"Would they indeed?" said Leeyes. "Sergeant Perkins makes a good nun, does she?"

Sergeant Perkins flushed. "That headdress thing ..."

"Coif," supplied Sloan, now the expert.

"Coif is about the most uncomfortable thing I've ever worn."

"You didn't wear her hair shirt then," said Leeyes acidly.

"No, sir. On the other hand, sir, you can't blame Ranby for making a mistake that first time. You can't see a nun's face unless you get a straightforward front view, you know, and I don't suppose he wanted to do that anyway."

"Don't forget either, sir," put in Sloan, "that nuns don't age as quickly as we do. I don't know why. But Sister Anne looked the sort of age he expected Sister Lucy to look by now."

"And," went on Sergeant Perkins, "it's about the darkest corridor I've ever been in."

"That's their subconscious harking back to candle-power," said Sloan *sotto voce*.

Leeyes ignored this. "So Ranby killed Sister Anne on Wednesday in error?"

"Pure and simple case of mistaken identity, sir. It all fits. He was out to kill Sister Lucy, the Bursar and Procuratrix, who always wears that great big heavy bunch of keys hanging from her girdle. Always."

"Except on Wednesday evenings?"

"No, just this one Wednesday so that Sister Anne could look out some gifts to send to the Missions in time for Christmas. I gather in the ordinary way she would have come with her, but she was busy on Wednesday evening."

"What's she got to be busy about?"

Sloan didn't know. He didn't think he would ever know what made them busy in a Convent. "Anyway, sir, she handed over her badge of office—a very conspicuous one—to Sister Anne, and so Ranby thinks it's her. He picks up the orb on the newel post ..."

"He knew all about that, did he?"

"Oh, yes, sir, from Celia Faine. He hits Sister Anne very hard indeed on the back of the head and puts it back. Not even bothering to wipe it very clean. If it's found it's a pointer to an inside job, isn't it?"

"It wasn't found," pointed out the superintendent unkindly. "Not until someone laid it out on a plate for you."

"No, sir," said Sloan. "On the other hand it didn't mislead us about its being an inside job either, did it? And then, sir," he went on hurriedly, not liking the superintendent's expression, "he bundles the body into the broom cupboard and takes the glasses off. It's quite dark in there too and so he still doesn't know he's nobbled the wrong horse."

"And then what?"

"He goes back to the Institute for supper."

"He does what?"

"Goes back to the Institute for supper."

"Who threw her down the stairs then?"

"He did."

"When?"

"After supper."

"Why?"

"Delay her being found, upset the timing, make us think she'd fallen—that sort of thing. Implicating Town, too, if necessary. It wouldn't have been any bother to drag her along the corridor and shove her down the steps as he was there anyway."

"How do you mean he was there anyway?"

"He came back after his own supper at the Institute," said Sloan, "to attend Vespers. He didn't want her found before the boys got to the Convent. He hadn't an alibi for a quarter to seven or thereabouts when he killed her, but if she was thought to be alive at nine when they went off to bed it would throw a spanner in the calculations."

"Are you trying to tell me, Sloan—not very clearly if I may say so— that Ranby came twice to the Convent on Wednesday night?"

"Yes, sir, I am. He came to the service that they have just before their supper as an ordinary worshipper—Benediction I think it's called—and probably waited behind afterwards. The nuns all go into the refectory at a quarter past six for their supper and he goes along the corridor, opens the cellar door, nips down for the habit, puts it on and comes back up into that corridor. Then comes the tricky bit. He has to wait for Sister Lucy to come along. He takes the orb down."

"Didn't anyone notice it had gone?"

"I doubt if they'd have missed anything, not even the kitchen stove, until the time came to use it. No, I think he just stood inside the broom cupboard until he saw her come along."

"She'd have to be alone," objected Leeyes doubtfully.

"Yes, she would, but don't forget that after supper they have their recreation. They're allowed to potter about a little at will. It was the only chance he took really—her not happening to come his way. But if she didn't he could always go looking for her."

"In the Convent?"

"It's not difficult to pass as a nun if you're in the habit. He's fair-skinned anyway, they can't see his hair, he's got his own black shoes and socks on, trousers wouldn't show and believe you me, sir, nuns are the least observant crowd of witnesses it has been my unfortunate lot to encounter. They seem to think it's a sin to notice anything. And the light's so bad you never get a really clear view of anything after daylight. Ranby never saw Sister Anne's face sufficiently well at any time to know it wasn't Sister Lucy. There's no light to speak of in the corridor itself, and he wouldn't dare shine a torch. That would be asking for trouble."

"So he kills Sister Anne, goes back to the Institute for supper ..."

"That's right, sir. They would notice if he weren't there anyway, but particularly at the Institute supper."

"Why?"

"There are fourteen resident staff all told, including Ranby, so if one is missing there are—"

"I can do *simple* arithmetic, Sloan."

"Yes, sir." Sloan coughed. "As soon as the supper at the Institute was finished I reckon he came back, put on the habit and Sister Anne's glasses. He only had to be last in to the Chapel to know which was her stall." He took a breath. "And he was—Sister Damien said so. Then he waits until the nuns have gone to bed, drags the body to the top of the cellar steps, throws it down, leaves the habit ready for Town, puts the glasses in his pocket, and goes back to his quarters in the Institute. I expect he rang for the maid to take away his coffee cup or sent for one of the staff or students—something like that to imply that he'd been there all the time. Nobody's likely to ask him any questions though, because he thought there was nothing to connect him with the Convent at all."

"But there was?"

"There must have been something or he wouldn't have had to kill Town."

"Ah, Town. I was forgetting Town." The superintendent never forgot anything.

"I think Town had to die because he saw something which connected Ranby with the Convent."

"What?"

Sloan tapped his notebook. "I'm not absolutely certain but I think I can guess."

"Well?"

"Ranby stepped out of that habit somewhere around nine-fifteen or nine-twenty after being inside it for nearly an hour. Town picked it up at nine-thirty."

"Well?"

"It would still be warm, sir. I think Town noticed."

"That crack about warm milk," burst out Crosby involuntarily.

Sloan nodded. "Ranby must have had good reason for thinking Town knew or guessed something. It would be easy enough for him to catch Town in between the study periods yesterday morning and tell him they were walking over to the Convent without the others." He shrugged his shoulders. "We'll never know what it was Town knew. Unless Ranby tells us. Mind you, sir, I don't think he will. The only thing he's said so far is 'Get me my solicitor.' "

"Much good that'll do him," said the superintendent. "You've got him cold, I hope."

"I hope so," echoed Sloan piously, "but it's a long story."

The superintendent sighed audibly. "Suppose you go back to the beginning ..."

"There are really two beginnings, sir."

"One will do very nicely, Sloan. Let's have the earliest first."

"That was twelve years ago, sir, in West Laming. Where Sergeant Gelden went last night."

Sergeant Gelden nodded corroboratively.

"It concerns two people," said Sloan, "Mr. Marwin Ranby, then Deputy Headmaster of West Laming School, and a Miss Felicity Ferling, niece of Miss Dora Ferling of West Laming House. It was their both having come from West Laming that put me on to Ranby. This pair became very friendly indeed—Miss Ferling was a very charming, good-looking girl, greatly loved by her aunt who had brought her up. She became engaged to be married to this promising young schoolmaster and everything was arranged for the wedding. Two weeks before it Miss Dora Ferling had a visitor—Mr. Ranby's wife. He was already married. The wedding was abandoned, and Miss Felicity Ferling broken-hearted."

"So she took her broken heart to the Convent?"

"Not at first. They don't like women there for that reason, but apparently she'd always been very devout and interested in the life."

"He seems to like 'em that way," observed the superintendent. "Some men do. And the second beginning?"

"Ten days ago. At a public enquiry into the planning application to develop the land in between the Convent property and the Institute. Both sent representatives to it. The Institute sent Mr. Ranby and someone from the County Education Department. The Convent sent the Mother Superior and—"

"Don't tell me," said the superintendent. "I can guess."

"Sister Lucy—their Bursar. Just the worst possible time for her to turn up from Ranby's point of view. He's engaged again—this time to Miss Celia Faine, who stands a good chance of being wealthy if this development is allowed."

"Nasty shock for him—seeing his old flame sitting there."

"Very. And in nun's veiling too. Pretty impregnable places, convents."

"Ahah, I see where you're getting, Sloan."

"Exactly, sir. Ranby goes home to brood on ways and means."

"And his own students provide the answer?"

"That's right, sir. Plot Night in more ways than one. I think we shall find that Ranby either overheard or got to hear of the arrangement with Hobbett and seized his chance that night. The only other thing he needed to know was how to identify Sister Lucy without looking each nun in the face. A little judicious pumping of Hobbett would give him the answer to that, too—she always wore a great big bunch of keys. You'll have spotted the other misleading fact yourself, I'm sure, sir."

Leeyes growled noncommittally.

"Hobbett," went on Sloan, "doesn't know Sister Lucy doesn't wear glasses all the time. Any more than Ranby does. She would have been wearing them at the enquiry and when she paid Hobbett."

"You make it sound very simple," complained the superintendent.

"It was, sir. Motive, means and opportunity, the lot. He can't risk failure of a second attempt to marry a well-to-do unprotected girl—so there's the motive. The means are at hand—even down to the weapon—and his own students presented him with opportunity."

"Are you trying to tell me, Sloan, that Ranby can have gone to that Chapel with his future intended and those nuns not have known him from Adam?"

"Yes, sir. The Sisters sit in front of a grille, and the congregation would only ever see their backs. And," he added under his breath, "they none of them know Adam."

"What's that, Sloan?"

"Nothing, sir."

"I don't want any of your case based on false premise."

"No, sir." That was the course on Logic rearing its head again.

Leeyes turned to Crosby. "None of this 'when did you stop beating your wife' stuff, eh, constable?"

Crosby looked pained. "I'm not married, sir."

Harold Cartwright was still at The Bull.

"Fine woman, the Mother Superior. Makes me realize some of my ideas were a bit Maria Monk—you know, the Awful Disclosures thereof."

Sloan did not know, and said instead, "Any news of your father, sir?"

Cartwright shot him a sharp glance, "You knew, didn't you?"

"Yes, sir."

"He's much the same, Inspector, thank you. I'm going back home today but I'm coming back. ... Inspector Sloan?"

"Sir?"

"It was Ranby who sent for the police on Bonfire Night, wasn't it?"

"Yes, sir. I think he wanted us to see the habit and glasses just in case he had to pin something on someone else. After all, it wasn't very likely one nun would kill another really."

"And safer than throwing the glasses away."

"He was a bit too anxious to implicate the students. He suggested they might have got out of the Biology Laboratory window long before he was supposed to know what time they had gone to the Convent."

Cartwright gave his quick smile. "That job's still open for you, Inspector."

"No, thank you, sir, but there is one—what you might call—lost soul in need of one rather badly. A defector from St. Anselm's. I doubt if she's really employable myself."

"I could see," offered Cartwright.

"The name is Lome, Miss Eileen Lome. I'll give you her address."

"And I'll give you my London one."

Sloan coughed. "I have it, sir, thank you."

Cartwright nodded gravely. "I was forgetting. But I'll be coming back to The Bull. Funny thing you know, The Bull doesn't mean the animal at all."

"No, sir?"

"No. It means the Papal Bull. Isn't that odd? The Mother Superior told me."

Sloan went back to the car and tapped Crosby on the shoulder. "Get thee to a nunnery."

Sister Gertrude set off in the direction of the Parlor. There must be visitors there again. Usually Sister Lucy was sent for, but today Sister Lucy was being kept very busy by the Mother Superior on the question of the cost of a cloister. And this time they knew where the money was coming from. Mr. Harold Cartwright. Usually, when the Convent of St. Anselm spent some money they had no idea from whence the where-withal would appear. It always came, of course, but that was not easy to explain to a builder.

She hurried down the great staircase and wondered how long it would be before she could look at the newel post without a shudder. There was a portrait at the bottom of the stairs, framed and glass-covered. If you stood in a certain way you could catch sight of your own reflection. Sister Gertrude paused, squinted up at herself and pulled her coif quite straight.

Very wrong of her, of course. She would try not to do it again. But it was a temptation.

She joined the Mother Superior and went into the Parlor.

"So it was Mr. Ranby all the time," said the Mother Superior directly.

"Yes, marm," said Sloan. "He swallowed the bait—Sergeant Perkins—hook, line and sinker. If I may say so, Father MacAuley has a real talent for dissembling. Ranby never guessed the idea of the night watch was all a put-up job."

"Inspector, there is no doubt is there?"

"No, marm, we've found out other things too. He shaved twice that day and so on."

"Poor soul," she said compassionately, "to be so concerned with the passing things of this world."

"Yes, marm." He coughed. "Miss Faine … how …"

"Father MacAuley went to see her this morning after Mass. We must pray for her."

Sloan shifted uncomfortably in his chair. "Of course."

"The two boys from the Institute?" she enquired.

Sloan brightened. "They're taking it very well. It's quite taken their minds off Tewn."

"Inspector, when did you first suspect …?"

"Sister Lucy was white and shaking when I got here yesterday after you'd found Tewn's body. It wasn't that that had upset her because she hadn't seen it. What she had seen, of course, was Ranby. And Ranby had seen her and realized he'd killed the wrong Sister."

"He must have been a desperate man by last night."

"He was, marm. He tried to kill Sergeant Perkins. There was no doubt about that."

The Mother Superior inclined her head. "Sergeant Perkins is a courageous woman."

"In the course of duty, marm," he said hastily. It was a different discipline, a different dedication from that of the Sisters, but for all that it was still an equally dedicated way. "About Hobbett. …"

"In future," she said dryly, "he can ring for Sister Polycarp."

A bell suddenly echoed through the Convent. Both nuns rose, Sister Gertrude with a perceptible start. She had been wondering who it would be among the Community who would be bidden to move into the cell that had been Sister Anne's, the cell next to Sister St. Hilda the snorer. Was it wrong to pray God it wouldn't be her?

Sister Polycarp stumped to the door with the two policemen. "Good day, gentlemen. ..."

Was it Sloan's imagination or did she slam the grille behind them?

Crosby looked back at the Convent. "You wouldn't have thought, sir, would you, that after all that, it would turn out to be a *crime passionnel?*" He pronounced it "cream." "Not here."

"No," said Sloan shortly, "you wouldn't."

"That motto on the door, Inspector. ..."

"Well?"

"Do we really know what it means?"

Sloan turned on his heel and stared at the writing. "*Pax Intrantibus, Salus Exeuntibus.* Didn't you look it up, Crosby? You should have done. Very enlightening."

"Please sir ..."

"Peace to those who enter," translated Sloan. "Salvation to those who leave."

THE END

A Most Contagious Game
by Catherine Aird
978-1-60187-002-5
$14.95

When a heart attack forces Thomas Harding to retire with his wife Dora to a Tudor manor house in Calleshire County, he soon discovered that it comes complete with a priest hole, built by a clever Elizabethan crafts-man and containing—quite unfortunately—a skeleton from a much earlier time. Determined to learn more, Thomas begins to question the villagers, who are currently more concerned with the murder of a young wife and the disappearance of her well-liked husband. But in his efforts to solve a centuries-old crime, Thomas inadvertently contributes to the solution of the modern one and begins to take his place in the village of Easterbrook. First published in the U.S. in 1967.

About the Rue Morgue Press

"Rue Morgue Press is the old-mystery lover's best friend, reprinting high quality books from the 1930s and '40s."
—*Ellery Queen's Mystery Magazine*

Since 1997, the Rue Morgue Press has reprinted scores of traditional mysteries, the kind of books that were the hallmark of the Golden Age of detective fiction. Authors reprinted or to be reprinted by the Rue Morgue include Catherine Aird, Delano Ames, Morris Bishop, Dorothy Bowers, Pamela Branch, Joanna Cannan, Glyn Carr, Torrey Chanslor, Clyde B. Clason, Joan Coggin, Manning Coles, Lucy Cores, Frances Crane, Norbert Davis, Elizabeth Dean, Michael Gilbert, Constance & Gwenyth Little, Marlys Millhiser, Gladys Mitchell, James Norman, Stuart Palmer, Craig Rice, Kelley Roos, Charlotte Murray Russell, Maureen Sarsfield, Margaret Scherf, Juanita Sheridan and Colin Watson..

To suggest titles or to receive a catalog of Rue Morgue Press books write P.O. Box 4119, Boulder, CO 80306, telephone 800-699-6214, or check out our website, www.ruemorguepress.com, which lists complete descriptions of all of our titles, along with lengthy biographies of our writer